FINDING HOPE

SPARKS OF DESIRE

VALERIE TWOMBLY

DEDICATION

To those who have had or, currently have a toxic relationship. You are someone and you matter. Believe in yourself. Only you can make a change.
XOXO

ACKNOWLEDGMENTS

Many thanks to a special friend in the fire service. You not only check my fire scenes and offer excellent advice, you help push me for more. I couldn't do this without you.

Stay safe.

INTRODUCTION

Chance O'Connell doesn't do romance. After the firefighter has his heart broken, his idea of a relationship consists of one night with no attachments. Somehow, the dragon shifter finds himself drawn to Hope, the waitress at the local diner. Rather than make her one of his conquests, he sits in her section and pretends he doesn't want her.

Hope Sinclair is done with abusive men and being a victim. A new town and a new job at a local diner are all she needs for a fresh start. That is until a sexy firefighter takes up near residence in her section. He wants to be friends, but she wants something more. With the holiday bachelor auction coming up, Hope sets her heart on winning a date with Chance.

One night threatens Chance's vow to remain single, but by the time he finally admits they belong together, it might prove too late. Turns out Hope didn't run far enough and her past may be the end of them both.

1

Engines 31 and 32 rolled out of the station, sirens echoing into the cold, cloudy sky, and a shot of adrenaline pumped through Chance's veins. He lived for these moments. The opportunity to serve his community by saving property and most importantly, lives. For all the hell he'd seen in his years of service, every time he rescued a victim he was reminded why he was here. After strapping himself in, he glanced over at Derrick. "So, a wedding. I suppose I should bring a date."

Derrick gave him the side-eye. "Really? I figured you'd go solo so you could work your magic on all the single women. After all, I understand weddings are the best place to get laid."

Chance grinned. "Speaking from experience?"

"No comment," Derrick shot back. "Just remember, Halee will kick your ass from here to eternity if you embarrass her on her weddin' day."

"I wouldn't dream of it." He glanced out the window. "Besides, it's her father who scares the living fuck out of me."

"Cearul? He seems like a perfectly nice guy."

"Oh, sure he is, but ruin his daughter's wedding? You'll see what a several thousand year old shifter is capable of, and personally, I have no fucking desire to bear witness up close and intimate."

Derrick laughed. "I thought you were a dragon not a pussy."

"Funny, ha, ha."

Minutes later, Reese was situating them in front of a two-story house, fire on the upper floor. Cold Creek was one of the nicer subdivisions located on the edge of town. Its homes of ten years and slightly older were mostly wood frame construction, which meant they could be dealing with fire hidden inside the walls and attics.

"Chief's on site. Let's go," Gaelen said as he piled out of the passenger seat and headed to locate his brother Kadin, the chief of Station 3. Chance and Derrick jumped out and Chance grabbed a six-foot pike-pole from the engine and ran across the snow-covered lawn. Gaelen met him and Derrick halfway.

"Lines are going to the second floor. You guys get up there."

"Got it." Chance's internal clock kicked in as he dropped the pole, removed his left glove, shoving it between his knees, and pushed his helmet behind his head. The motions now etched into his memory, he pulled down and secured his mask, stretched his hood over his head, shoved his helmet back on and tightened the chin strap before he donned his glove. Picking up his pole, he glanced at Derrick, who had finished a nanosecond before him. This new technique had been courtesy of Derrick, who was able to mask up and be ready to enter a building in nine seconds. Kadin, their chief, had been thrilled with Derrick's training and the competition of who in the firehouse could mask up fastest had begun.

"A little slow on the uptake there, O'Connell." Derrick referred to Chance by his last name.

"Next time, I'll kick your Texas ass, Taylor."

Derrick laughed. "Bring it on."

Chance made his way to the front door where he ran into Devin on the nozzle and Torin trailing him, dragging in a charged line. Chance took the stairs with Derrick behind him. At the top, Asher loomed in a doorway, busy shoving aside charred debris.

Fire tore through the room.

"We need a fucking line up here," Ash shouted.

"On its way." Chance moved into a bedroom across the hall, looking at the ceiling as he went. He spotted a basketball-sized hole and the telltale orange glow that indicated fire. As he walked through the room, he spotted a second hole on the other side.

"Hey, we got fire. We got fire through the entire attic," he shouted and began jabbing the pole into the ceiling. Once he had an opening, he started ripping down drywall. Burning chunks rained to the floor.

"Hey, I got ya a hole." He walked back into the hall where the rest of the crew had punched holes into the ceiling, and Devin was on the nozzle, spraying water into the attic. "I got a hole in the bedroom."

"Another line is on the way up," Torin answered.

Chance spotted one of the guys shoving a nozzle at Derrick, who grabbed it and headed back down the hall. Chance moved to his friend's back.

"Hey, give me more line," Derrick shouted.

"More line," Chance yelled and the words echoed down the stairs as men repeated the command. Soon Chance was pulling more hose so Derrick could get into the room and start putting water into the attic.

Evan jumped in behind Derrick to help support the line and Derrick's back. Nothing made your muscles scream more than hosing over your head.

"Let me get you more holes," Chance said as Derrick continued to spray. He grabbed his bar and started pulling the ceiling ahead of the water stream. Chunks of burning debris dropped and bounced off his helmet, singeing the carpet beneath his boots. Water cascaded off his shoulders.

"Hey, I'm gonna look at pulling that fucking corner." He pointed to the other side of the room then proceeded. Jamming his hook into the ceiling, he pulled more drywall and the roar of flames greeted him. "We've got heavy fire over here."

Derrick advanced with the hose and began dousing the flames. Water slicked the floor where there was no carpet and ran across the room. Chance stepped over charred chunks of wood and burning ceiling to make his way back across the room. He was looking for hot spots kicking up where they had already doused the fire.

"Taylor, hit it here." Chance pointed into the rafters now exposed to the mid-day sky. They were actually lucky the roof had burned through. It helped not only bring in some much needed light but kept the smoke from curling down around them.

Derrick shut down his line. "I'm sitting at twenty minutes." It was time for him to get out. His tank would soon be nearing the empty mark.

Someone's PASS alarm went off then quickly quieted. A common occurrence Chance always paid attention to. He'd heard too many horror stories about the alarms being ignored out of habit only to later discover a fellow firefighter had been in trouble.

Not on his damn watch. Never.

Chance took the nozzle from Derrick. "Get out. We've almost got this."

With three hoses going, the last of the fire quickly abated, and soon the men were heading down the stairs and outside.

Chance helped with clean up while Torin and Ash grabbed garbage bags and headed back in to collect clothing for the residents who were huddled across the street at a neighbor's house. While their home could not be occupied, it was salvageable and everyone had gotten out. A young boy ran up to him, holding a thermos and a pack of Styrofoam cups.

"My mom said I could bring you coffee."

Chance squatted so he was eye level with the boy. "What's your name?" He accepted the gift of a hot drink.

"Brandon."

"You doing okay, Brandon?"

The boy nodded. "Yeah. I remembered what you guys taught us when you came to my school, and I made sure we all got out when the smoke detector went off."

"God job and thanks for the coffee."

"You're welcome. I better get back to my mom." Then he ran across the street, his mother's watchful eye on him every second.

Chance smiled, thankful he hadn't been forced to pull the small boy from his burning home.

Today was a victory.

———

Hope wiped down a table and looked up at the clock on the diner wall.

"You have looked at that thing a hundred times," Bea said from behind the counter as she placed freshly baked pies into the glass case for the dinner crowd.

"I can't help it."

"You're going to scrub the finish right off that table too."

Hope stopped wiping and straightened. Her back hurt and her feet screamed a warning to take a break or else. She walked to a stool at the counter and sat down. Bea poured her a cup of coffee and slid a slice of cherry pie in front of her.

"Here, eat this. You have hours to kill before tonight's auction."

She groaned then took a bite of pie. "Bea, your pies are always fabulous." She emptied a packet of sugar into her mug and dribbled in creamer, stirring until it was a rich tan.

"You need to stop worrying. I'm sure you'll win tonight's bachelor auction." Bea came around the counter with her own cup of coffee. This was the quiet before the dinner crowds showed up so they would both take advantage of it. Bea was the owner of Kirkwood Diner, often cooking and sometimes waiting tables. The woman was a good soul.

The auction she referred to was held every year a week before Thanksgiving when all the eligible firefighters auctioned one date for charity. Hope had had a crush on Chance O'Connell since the day she laid eyes on him two years ago. He came into the diner for breakfast when he was working at the firehouse. She'd done everything to get noticed, but while he was always kind, it had been no more than that. Tonight, she was going to enter the bidding war for a single date with him, in hopes he would see her as more than just the girl who brought him his breakfast and listened to his stories.

Faith might spring eternal.

"I am a firm believer that if a couple is meant to be together, nothing will stop that from happening." Bea broke Hope's thoughts.

"Maybe I'm being silly. I mean, what do I really know about Chance?" Other than he didn't really date. He was a man who liked to play the field and play it he did.

"That he is what a lady's fantasies are made of?"

Hope laughed. Bea had been widowed a year before Hope had moved to Minnesota and come to the diner to answer the help wanted ad. The two had hit it off immediately.

"Sounds like someone might need a date herself," Hope laughed.

Bea sipped her coffee while Hope polished off the slice of pie.

"I'm not above admitting I have a special friend." She smiled. "With benefits."

"Oh my God!" Hope lowered her voice. "Good for you. I wish I had your balls."

Bea rose and picked up the empty plate. "When you get to be my age, you stop caring what others think and go for what you want. You'd do well to heed that advice now. Whether you win or lose at tonight's auction, make Chance notice the true woman you are. He'll come around soon enough." Then she went to the kitchen and left Hope with a lot to think about.

Rising from her stool, the bell rang indicating a customer had entered. When she turned, she found herself face-to-face with the man who had spent many nights in her bed. Well, in her dreams at least. He appeared weary yet offered a smile as he took a spot in the booth.

"Hi, Chance. You on duty?" While he was in uniform, he was also here later than usual.

"Yeah. I missed breakfast and lunch but didn't feel like hanging at the station."

"Out on a call? I hope no one was hurt." She didn't know how the guys and gals of their local fire department did it but was thankful they did.

"Yeah. Everyone got out, but their home will need a lot of work before they can move back in."

"That's tough, especially at the holidays, but at least no lives were lost."

He gave a nod before he opened his mouth and stunned her with what he said next. "You ever think of settling down and having a family?" This from the one-and-done guy?

"I... I've thought about it often. Just haven't met the right guy." She decided to go with the flow and see where this conversation led. "You?"

He shrugged. "I'd like kids one day, but love's overrated."

Well hell. Not the answer she wanted to hear, but then again what did she expect? Hope was forever picking the wrong guy to fall for. Even with that knowledge, she wasn't about to be deterred in tonight's bidding.

2

Chance paced, hidden behind the blue-curtained stage at Kirkwood High School. Mrs. Williams, the school principal, stood front and center painting prose about Reese Durham and his many fine qualities. Reese was the station's engine driver and had been with Station 3 for the last ten years. However, he'd only been attending the Five Alarm Bachelor Auction for the past three. Reese had been almost inconsolable when his wife of ten years picked up and left one day, saying she was in love with someone else. Namely Reese's own brother. The poor bastard had taken to drinking heavily and had been on the verge of being suspended from his job. Chance had taken him aside and told him to get his shit together. During that time, the two grew close. Chance even confided his own heart-breaking past and somehow helped Reese get back on his feet while Reese, in turn, helped Chance realize life went on. That's when the friendly competition started between the two. They both went all out every year, trying to beat the other and bring in the highest bid. The official Kirkwood Five Alarm Bachelor Auction was the highlight of the community, bringing much needed funds and a healthy rivalry between the three firehouses, as well as the Wildland crews.

"I think you should lose the shirt."

Chance glanced over his shoulder and raised a brow at Isabella Murphy. Bella, as everyone called her, worked the other shift as a paramedic.

"How come we've never hooked up?" he inquired. After all, Bella was a beautiful female with sun-kissed brown hair and curves in all the right places.

She laughed. "First, you assume I'd ever date you, and second, that my brothers wouldn't kill you after."

True, there was that. Kadin, the patriarch of the Murphy family, was a shifter like Chance but much older. Kadin had recently been hellbent on getting the eldest Murphy sister––who just happened to be a full-blooded shifter––to mate with one of their own. He'd failed miserably when Halee instead fell in love with one of their newest firefighters, Derrick Taylor. Derrick was one hundred percent human and definitely not Kadin's first choice. However, Kadin had come around. Now the man was busy harassing the youngest sibling, Bella.

"You're right. Kadin would probably kill me and my body would never be found."

"Most likely become fodder for some starving farm animals." Her mouth turned into a smirk before she broke out in laughter. "Cow cud." She slapped her thigh and snorted.

"You are fucking hysterical." He moved his attention back to the stage where the bidding was furiously taking place. The ladies were already up to five hundred for a date with Reese. Bella sidled up next to him.

"I'm telling you. Shirt off and you will kick ass. Show the ladies that eight pack you're hiding under there."

He grinned and pushed his suspenders off then got rid of the tee he'd put on earlier. What the hell, he would walk out on stage in his underwear if it meant he kicked Reese's ass.

"I'll wager a hundred bucks that I'll take both of you down tonight." Gaelen sauntered up wearing a black tux, crisp white shirt, and a dark purple tie. "Ladies like a well-dressed man."

"Brother!" Bella kissed Gaelen on the cheek. "If we weren't related, I would bid on you myself. You look amazing!"

Gaelen slipped on a pair of dark sunglasses and Chance rolled his eyes.

"Fucker, you're on. Hundred bucks says you can't take me."

"Wow, I think it's gonna be war between you three." Bella looked between her brother and Chance. "May the best bachelor bring in top dollar. The community really needs it this year."

After a fire that demolished the local mill, many families had been left out of work while the company rebuilt. Thankfully, Kirkwood had some families with money to spare, and many of them were in the audience tonight bidding on a date with one of the bachelor firefighters from the three stations in town.

"Sweet! Reese just closed out at eight hundred," Bella said.

Reese sauntered across the stage, his grin wide as he brushed past them. "Chance, you're up. See if you can top eight hundred."

Chance straightened. "I'm about to kick your ass. By the way, Gaelen and I have a wager going if you care to join in."

"I'm happy to take your money. Count me in," Reese said.

"Bella, you're the keeper of the records. I don't have any cash on me at the moment."

"Oh, don't worry your pretty little heads off, boys. I'll make sure you all pay up," she laughed.

Chance looked into the audience. "Ladies, prepare to be dazzled." Then he stepped out from behind the curtain.

———

Hope's palms sweated so much she had to keep wiping them on her jeans. When Chance finally sauntered across the stage, her breath caught in her lungs.

Jesus take the wheel because this car was about to wreck.

Chance had decided to wear only his turnout pants and boots. Even his suspenders hung at his side, giving every lady in the small gym a view that would put a smile on their face until their dying day.

Hot wasn't even a word to describe him, and when he turned to offer a glimpse of his backside—a back that was sculpted to perfection—Bea Turner, who sat to her right, gasped.

"Lord have mercy." The woman fanned herself with the paper auction number. "Honey, now that man would make a fine friend with benefits. I think the bidding is about to go nuclear."

Hope chewed her lip. Bea knew how much this night meant to Hope. It had been difficult to hide the growing crush she had on Chance O'Connell from the older woman. Bea would often wait tables because she loved being around the customers, and when Chance came in, Bea would wink and make sure Hope waited on him.

"I've been saving." She had, but she'd also cashed in some stock a year ago that had threatened to dive. It had been a good thing too because the company had suddenly folded. Her brother, who handled her finances, said the CEO skimmed off profits. Whatever, she wasn't into watching the stock market and was thankful her brother Eric took care of her money. Right now, the town of Kirkwood was in dire need of cash that these fundraisers brought in. If she could kill two birds by winning a date with Chance, as well as help her neighbors, she was all over it. Maybe spending time with Chance without all the other distractions would finally make him notice she was a living, breathing woman. Either way, the town would get her money because if she did lose, she still planned to donate the funds.

The bidding started at one hundred. Hope held up her number and shouted. "Two hundred!"

"Oh, you go get him," Bea said, a glint of mischief in her eye.

Another female yelled out. "Four hundred!"

Oh hell no!

Chance strutted, yelling back, "Come on ladies. An evening of this"—he waved his hands over his chest—"and dinner of your choice." He stopped front and center. "I'm a damn good cook, or if you prefer, I'm happy to take you to the nicest place in the city."

Hope preferred home cooking, thank you very much. "Five hundred!" She waved her card to be sure she was seen.

Mrs. Williams spoke into the microphone. "Ladies, did you know that Chance has kindly offered to match his winning bid tonight? What a wonderful gesture. We are currently at five hundred."

"Seven hundred," her competition screamed.

Hope's heart beat against her ribs. She couldn't lose, and it didn't appear to matter how much she flirted, Chance wasn't going to ask her out. "One thousand!"

The crowd cheered and Mrs. Williams smiled. "I have one thousand. Can I get one thousand-one hundred?"

Her breathing stopped as she waited, praying for the winning bid to come her way.

"One thousand and two hundred," a persistent female shouted out that Hope wanted to strangle.

Taking a deep breath, she swallowed. Screw this, she was going all in. "One thousand, five hundred." She never had been one to do things half-assed.

Bea touched Hope's arm. "Nice move. No sense in fooling around."

Hope clutched the paper number in her hand so hard it crinkled as Mrs. Williams continued to try and get the bid higher. The crowd whispered, no doubt wondering how a gal waiting on tables could come up with so much money. She'd never really shared her past, other than to tell people she had moved from the Big Apple. When asked why, she simply replied she'd grown tired of city life. In reality, she had run from a nightmare she hoped never to relive again.

"Sold to the highest bidder for one thousand and five hundred dollars." Mrs. Williams pulled Hope from her thoughts.

"You won, dear. How exciting!" Bea leaned closer. "If I were you, I would take him up on that home cooked meal." The woman winked.

That was definitely her plan. She didn't want to share Chance with anyone. It was the only way she would have his undivided attention. Hope got up and made her way to the aisle so she could get to the lobby and pay for her prize. A few minutes later, she was handing the gal behind the table one hundred dollar bills and collecting her receipt.

"I need you to fill out this contact information so your date can reach you to set things up." The girl smiled as she handed Hope a pen and a card on a clipboard. Hope accepted then moved to a vacant chair to fill it out. A few minutes later, she'd turned it back in and headed home. It was late and she had an early shift at the diner. Not that she would be able to sleep tonight. No, she would be busy dreaming about the tall, blond-haired, blue-eyed, dreamy firefighter she'd just won a date with.

———

C hance was jerked from a sound sleep by the screaming alarm. He leaped from bed and pulled on his tee as he hurried from his bunk to the bathroom. Damn, now he wished he hadn't drank that giant soda earlier. It was no easy task to piss while the fire alarm was screaming in his ear, and time was of the essence. Finally, he managed to get the job done and headed to the bay where he slipped on his turnout gear then climbed into the engine.

Reese slid into the driver seat, and they were soon joined by Torin and Asher.

"I'm surrounded by you fucks," Reese said as he drove from the bay and into the street, lights and sirens blaring.

Torin, who sat in the front, chuckled. "You love us."

Reese only grumbled. Chance supposed being the only human in the engine might be intimidating, but Reese had been around long enough to handle anything they had to dish out.

"He's just pissed I beat his ass in the bachelor auction," Chance added.

Ash snorted. "Dude, you kicked everyone's ass. Damn, but fifteen hundred? I wouldn't pay ten cents to date your stinky ass."

"And I wouldn't fuck you with Reese's dick," Chance retorted.

Reese mumbled obscenities under his breath, but before anyone else responded, their expert driver positioned them several feet away from the burning car. Time to get serious.

Everyone jumped from the engine and assessed the situation. Luckily, no one was trapped inside because the entire front of the

Camaro was on fire. Chance grabbed the line and walked to the vehicle, untwisted a kink as he slung it to the side, pulled down his visor then turned the nozzle.

"Son of a bitch. I could piss faster than this," he muttered before shouting over his shoulder. "Crank it up!"

The engine hummed louder and a second later Chance twisted the nozzle again. This time he had full pressure and began hosing the hood, working his way toward the front passenger compartment where Ash had jerked open the driver door. Cold wind dipped from the north, and a light snow started to fall. While he doused the flames, he noticed Gaelen had shown up in his personal truck and was pulling blankets from the back seat. Their captain offered them to the young couple standing on the sidewalk shivering. The guy was wearing a pair of jeans and a suit jacket that likely belonged to his dad, while his date had stuffed herself into a short dress that looked like it had been poured over her. The two couldn't be more than seniors in high school, and Chance wondered if her father had seen her leave the house in that getup. He cringed at the thought one day he might have a daughter who'd be dating.

Over his dead damn body.

As the flames finally started to give up the fight, he wondered if maybe it wasn't time for him to consider giving up as well and settle down. Since he'd lost Mia, he had gone from woman to woman and gained the reputation of one-and-done. Refusing to ever give his heart again. However, recently desires had stirred. More than sexual, they were soul deep and he didn't understand them. He often went to the local diner for breakfast only to catch a glimpse of Hope. Her laughter soothed his internal beast, and he swore the dragon actually purred. Hope scared him though. She was everything good, much like Mia and look how that had ended. With him hugging Mia's broken body as he watched her take her last breath. The terror in her eyes would live with him forever.

Finally, the fire inside the car was out and a burnt shell was all that remained. Ash wandered to the hood and wedged a porta-power between the frame then engaged the switch. Metal groaned before it busted the latch with a loud bang, and Ash was able to lift the hood. A small flicker of flames remained, which Chance quickly doused.

A city plow drove by and tossed salt on the wet, freezing pavement as the crew cleaned up. The snow came down harder, but he didn't mind. Shifters loved the cold. It was why many of them lived in the north. He kept the flow going on the hose until the last of the water trickled out then began to roll it up and place it back on the engine.

"Fuck, it's cold out here." Reese smacked his hands together and rubbed.

"You're a pussy. It's a beautiful night."

Reese scowled. "I will admit this is the one time I'm jealous of you guys. Cold has no effect on your scaly ass."

Reese was right about that. Chance's ancestors were from the Wicklow Mountains of Ireland, and they thrived in the cold weather. "Then I guess we'd better get you back to the station and tucked into bed before you freeze to death."

"I was thinking we could all pool some money together and get him a couple pairs of those footie jammies," Ash laughed.

Reese tried to flip them off with his heavy gloves. "Fuck all of you. At least I won't live for centuries. I can't imagine watching my kids go before me."

"That only happens if the girl mates a human." Gaelen jumped into the conversation.

"So, that's why Kadin's now after Bella?" Reese sighed. "I just can't imagine watching my little Emma pass before me."

"Maybe your little girl will grow up and marry a shifter." Torin had been quiet all evening. Well, until he tossed that small bomb out. Chance searched Reese's face, expecting the man to lose his shit.

"I might harass you guys, and it may be difficult for me to grasp your reality, but there is one thing I do know about your kind. When you choose the woman you wish to mate with, it's forever. If my Emma was lucky enough to find love among your kind, I wouldn't stand in her way." His brows dipped. "But don't get any ideas. I don't think I could handle any of you dating my daughter when she's grown. That's just fucked up." He shook his head and walked away.

Chance watched his friend climb back into the engine.

"I think he needs to get laid. That ex of his did a damn number on him," Ash said.

"Yeah, she did indeed. Reese was supposed to have his daughter for Thanksgiving, but looks like that's not happening now," Chance replied, and in the back of his mind, he wished his friend could find some kind of happiness. Hell, they all could use a little joy this holiday season.

3

Hope had just finished wiping down the table when Chance strolled in and kicked her pulse up several notches. He looked as good in a pair of faded jeans as he had in his fire pants the other night. His dark blond hair was perfect, and she wondered if he ever had a hair out of place. A sudden desire to slide her fingers through it and give him an unkempt look had her clenching her fists. His deep blue eyes met hers.

"Morning, Hope."

"Morning, Chance. The usual today?"

He scratched his chin. "I need a change in my life. Might as well start with breakfast." He took a seat at the booth she'd just cleaned.

"Really? Was it a bad night?" Ever since she had come to work at the Kirkwood Diner, Chance had the same breakfast whenever he came in.

"Naw, just a car fire. No casualties thankfully. Maybe it's the upcoming holidays that have me in a mood."

Perfectly understandable. She pulled out her pad and pen. "Well then, what will it be?"

He tapped his fingers on the table as if he were nervous, and she was beginning to wonder what was wrong with him. Could he have jitters about their date? After all, she had been the highest bidder and he'd yet to mention it. She quickly brushed it aside. Chance was not a man who would be skittish about a date. Not if the rumors she heard about him were true. Bea had warned her that Chance liked to frequent the city and had not had a steady girlfriend.

Ever.

While Hope walked into this with that knowledge, she believed maybe he simply hadn't met who he was searching for. Did she imagine she was that woman? She wasn't so stupid to think so but would love an opportunity to get to know the real man instead of the projected a facade.

"What's your favorite?" He looked up and smiled, nearly melting her into a puddle of goo.

Pull yourself together, girl! Hope wasn't normally like this. Especially considering her last boyfriend, but her gut said Chance was different. Of course, she had been wrong before.

"I'm rather fond of the waffle with strawberries and a side of bacon."

"Huh. Sounds more like dessert, but I'm willing to try it."

"In your case, I'd also recommend a side of eggs." Bea had told Hope when she started waitressing, and the firefighters began trickling in for breakfast, that many of them were shifters. Even pointed out who was what in this case. Hope had been intrigued. To her knowledge, she'd never met a real shifter and her curiosity was piqued. Actually, she wondered what one would be like in the bedroom, and her cheeks heated at the thought.

God, had it really been two years since she'd had sex? Even then, what she'd had with David didn't count. He'd always been more interested in his own needs.

"Whatever you think."

"I'll go put in your order." She needed a minute to regain her composure and definitely had to stop thinking those kinds of thoughts. Hell, she should stop thinking all together. It was dangerous, yet she was unable to. Hope was wise enough to realize not all men were like David. Realized it because she had dated others before him. Hope was a firm believer in giving everyone a fair shake until they proved they didn't deserve her trust. Yet, she was also smart enough to keep a wall around her heart.

As she walked away and put in Chance's order, she asked herself one hard question. What did she really want from the sexy firefighter? A friend? A night of passion or was it more than that? Grabbing the coffee pot and a mug, she headed back to his table with no real answer to her burning question.

Just see how this one date goes then decide. But that brought up a whole new set of issues. What if he made a move on her? Her body screamed to jump on that horse and ride it until he begged her for mercy. Her mind screamed she was a good girl and that would be a bad move.

Damn the sensible side of her anyway.

She poured his coffee. "Your food will be up soon." Started to walk away when he grabbed her wrist. Such a simple touch sent fire through her veins and desire spreading to her nether region. Yep, the naughty side was wide awake now.

"You got a second?" He looked around as if checking to see how many customers there were. At the moment, he was the only one in her section.

"Of course."

"So, I understand you're the winning bidder. That was a lot of money."

"It was nothing and the town will benefit."

"Very kind of you. So, where would you like to go?"

She swallowed down the words, *to your bed*. "I rather liked the offer of you cooking for me." Images of him wearing only an apron flashed through her mind, and the heat in her cheeks matched the rest of her body.

Damn it, Hope, get it together!

"I love to cook. How about this Saturday?"

"That would be perfect. Can I bring dessert?"

"Sure. It's a date then." He whipped out a pen while she tore a blank ticket from her pad and handed it to him. "Come over about seven." He jotted his address and phone number then handed it to her. "You know how to get there?"

She looked at the paper. Laurel Lane, she'd heard of it but had never been there. "I can find it. Your breakfast is up. I'll be right back." She shoved the paper in her pocket and headed for the back, her step much lighter than before.

———

Chance studied the sway of her hips as she walked away. Hope was a beautiful woman, and he was happy she had won the date. He certainly could have done worse. Dinner with one of the old ladies in town would have proved to be a long, painful evening. At least with Hope, he knew they could carry on a conversation, and since he always enjoyed their banter when he came into the restaurant, he might actually like getting to know her better. Correction, he had wanted to get to know her better since he'd first laid eyes on her. His own fears had held him back.

Moments later, she was back and setting two plates in front of him. One with scrambled eggs and several strips of bacon. The other, a large, round waffle covered with strawberries and whipped cream.

"Definitely looks like a woman's breakfast."

"Oh, hush up and try it. It's even better with the bacon on top."

He glanced up and laughed at her. Hope had never been afraid to speak her mind, and he liked that about her. "Well, now you're talking my language." He followed her advice and broke up a piece of bacon, crumbling it over the waffle then took a bite. The crispness of the waffle, along with the subtle sweetness of the berries and saltiness of bacon, turned out to be an awesome combination. "Wow. I have to admit, that's pretty damn good."

Hope raised her chin. "I do know a little about food. Holler if you need anything else." She topped off his coffee then went to help a couple who had just taken a seat. Chance finished his breakfast then pulled out his wallet, tossing a wad of cash on the table. As he got up to leave, Hope walked past again.

"See you Saturday," he said.

"I'm looking forward to having someone else cook for me." She smiled and he laughed. It would be nice and different spending an evening with a woman he wasn't looking to get into bed. Not that Hope didn't stir his male desires, she definitely did. He wanted to know how she felt beneath him, but Hope was the wholesome girl next door who deserved a man so much better than him. So why did he seem to have this infatuation with the diner waitress?

Walking out the door, he considered his life. He went from woman to woman, searching for something he never found. What was he looking for? Another female that would look at him with fear when she learned what he really was? Mia had done that. Even after swearing she loved him more than anything, she fled when he showed her what he was. Struck by a car, he had watched her life fade away, and it had been all his fault.

As he slid into his truck and pulled it into gear, he wondered what Hope would think about his dragon. Would she run in fear? For some reason, the thought of those hazel eyes reflecting terror back at him made his heart sink. Pulling into the street, he headed for home and reminded himself why he never allowed any woman to get close. Why he held no desire for a white picket fence. He had promised that life to another long ago. A woman who held his heart in her hands, and then had crushed it. So why was he considering something more with Hope?

Because the dragon wanted what it wanted, and it desired the female who had been out of reach for the last two years.

———

Hope took a step back and scanned her bedroom. Clothes she had tried on then rejected were discarded all over the room. "What a mess and I'm still not dressed." She glanced at the clock on her nightstand, which currently mocked her with its red numbers.

Only twenty minutes left before she would have to be out the door and on the road.

Blowing out a deep breath, she slipped on a pair of skinny jeans. At least she liked how they made her backside look. "Okay, I'm halfway there." Next, she pulled on a white stretchy tank then donned a soft, light pink sweater that hung off her shoulder. Last came the low-heel black boots that she zipped over her jeans before stepping back to look in the mirror.

"Not bad for someone who's forty." A quick brush through her brown locks, a spritz of perfume, and a touch up of her lip gloss, and she was as ready as she was ever going to get. Exiting the bedroom, she flipped off the light and scooped up Harley then headed into the kitchen.

"It's just you and the radio tonight, buddy. Momma has a date." The little maltipoo licked her chin then let out a yap, causing her to laugh. "I know, shocking isn't it?" She placed the dog on the floor and picked up his water bowl. Dumping the contents into the sink, she gave it a quick rinse and filled it with fresh water.

"You better go out and do your business." Walking to the sliding door, she opened it and watched Harley run across the deck and down the path she'd shoveled for him earlier. While the dog was doing his thing, she grabbed the dessert off the counter. The chocolate raspberry ganache cake was thin layers of dark chocolate cake with dark chocolate ganache. Add to those heavenly layers, silky mascarpone and raspberry jam, and with every sinful bite, you entered a state of bliss.

She hoped Chance liked it. Hell, she was desperate for him to like her as well. Feelings of anxiety and inadequacy had her taking a deep breath. Too many times she had heard the hateful words...

"No man wants you, Hope. I'm all you've got."

Except she knew it wasn't true. She didn't deserve the treatment David had given her.

Hope placed some towels inside a box and nestled the cake between them. Going to the garage, she set the box on the passenger floor. By then Harley was waiting at the door, and when she let him back in, he scurried across the floor and curled up in his bed.

"What's the matter, are you cold?" She chuckled and grabbed her coat and purse. "Keep an eye on things, I'll be back later." She gave the dog one last scratch on his head before heading out. After getting settled into the driver's seat, she pulled up the GPS on her phone and waited for it to give directions.

"Deep breath, Hope. You're about to step into the dragon's lair."

Literally.

Backing out of the garage, she headed down the street until she hit the edge of town where her GPS told her to take a right. Hope was thankful it wasn't snowing and the roads were clear. Even though she had all-wheel drive, the climb up the winding logging road made her nervous. She was careful to keep an eye out for any wildlife. The last thing she wanted was to hit another living creature. It was more worry for the animal than herself. She had a soft spot for all creatures and hated those TV commercials that featured abused animals with the sad song playing in the background. It undid her every time.

Twenty minutes later, the GPS directed her to turn onto Laurel Lane. The street twisted through thick forest, but every so often she caught a glimpse of a large home. Many times, all she saw was a driveway that led to what she imagined was a glorious house at the end of it. When she reached the end of the street, she pulled into the only driveway there was and followed it for at least a quarter of a mile.

"Sheesh, this is a lane, not a driveway." When the house came into view, it was highlighted by a wash of soft light that cascaded over the wooden timbers of a two-story log home. She slowed to a crawl so she could take in as much as possible. Even though it was nearly seven in the evening, the property basked in the glow of the floodlights. When she pulled up to the garage and put the SUV into park, the side door opened and Chance stepped out. Bea's words from the other night came back to pass across her lips.

"Lord have mercy."

4

C hance heard the vehicle coming down the lane well before it appeared. Right on time. He liked that since he'd discovered women tended to be late.

He was at the door and had it open before she even exited the SUV. Hope opened the driver door and hopped out.

"Do you need help?" He stepped onto the sidewalk and started for her.

"If you wouldn't mind, dessert is on the other side."

Before she even got her door closed, he scooped the cake from the passenger side. "Chocolate?"

She batted golden hazel eyes at him as he rounded the front of her vehicle. "How did you know?"

"Superior sense of smell and a love for all things chocolate."

She laughed and followed him into the house. "Nice place you have. I didn't realize you were this far out of town."

"You can hang your coat in that closet there then come into the kitchen." He headed through the living room and placed the cake on the counter.

"Wow," she called out. "Something smells really good."

"Baked ziti with meatballs."

Hope walked into the kitchen, and he tried to keep his gaze from roaming over her curves. The way her jeans hugged her hips and the sweater left a shoulder exposed had him wishing she'd worn a sack. He managed to pull himself out of his thoughts. "Wine?"

"Oh, yes please." She moved to lean against the island. Her hip cocked out had him biting his lip. "This is an amazing kitchen. I've always dreamed of a big kitchen to bake in." She laughed again and he liked Hope's laugh. It was real, unlike many people he knew who were simply faking their way through life. On some days, he might even be one of them. He poured a glass of Merlot and handed it to her then raised his own.

"To the women of our community who come together every year and donate to a worthy cause." He touched his glass to hers then sipped.

"To the men who offer to be auctioned off like cattle."

He broke into laughter. "It's all in good fun."

"I'm not sure I could strut across the stage like that. I'd be afraid no one would bid."

"Hope, I can't imagine you would ever have to fear that." He glanced at the timer. "We've got about thirty minutes, shall we go have a seat?"

"Sure."

She followed him across the wooden floor to the living room. The fire he'd started earlier cast a warm glow over her face as she chose a seat next to it.

"I've always wondered what one of these big log homes looked like on the inside." Her gaze darted around the room.

"How about after dinner I give you a tour?"

"I'd like that." She settled back into the couch, and he took a seat in a chair across from her and swore disappointment flashed briefly across her face. He remembered back to a few months ago when Derrick had tried to tell Chance that Hope had the hots for him. He'd only laughed and thought Derrick was crazy. Had Chance somehow missed the signs or had he simply been ignoring them? He certainly never thought of Hope as someone who might go out with him. She was committed relationships and white picket fences. Then again, he hadn't wanted a real relationship since Mia. Now, he wasn't so sure what the hell he wanted.

"So, why did you become a firefighter?" She broke him free of his thoughts.

He lifted a shoulder. "I'm not really sure. It was something I kinda fell into and found I loved it. I guess it started when I pulled a neighbor out of their burning home several years back."

"How long have you been in?"

"About twenty years. After the incident with my neighbor, I joined the closest fire academy. I worked at a station in Wisconsin for three years when Kadin happened to tour the facility. Being a shifter, he knew immediately that I was as well and asked me to come join him here in Kirkwood. I've been here ever since." He studied her for any reaction to the admission of being a shifter. Hell, most of Kirkwood knew what they were and accepted them, but he wasn't sure Hope had ever been told. Not even her heart rate increased. Good sign.

"Amazing."

"What about you?" He noticed she glanced away at the question.

"I moved here from New York City about two years ago."

"Big difference, going from city life to northern Minnesota."

She took a big gulp of wine and twirled a strand of hair around her finger. It only made him want to shove his fingers into the thick brown mass and find out if it was as silky as it appeared.

"You don't have to tell me. Obviously, you're uncomfortable." Her breathing had increased as did her heart rate. All evidence she was distressed, and he suddenly wanted to know why.

———

Hope fought the panic. Talking about her past was difficult, but she also knew it was part of healing. None of it had been her fault and for some reason, staring into the blue eyes of the man across from her gave her courage. She wanted him to understand the horrors she'd survived. Hope refused to bury her past because when you did that it came back to take a chunk out of your soul.

"It was a big change, but I love this community." No lie there. She hadn't realized how much she would *not* miss her life back home.

"I left because of my ex."

"Ex-husband?"

She shook her head. "No. Boyfriend, but we did live together. Believe it or not, I had a beautiful apartment and a wonderful job I loved as a makeup artist for a small modeling agency, but I couldn't get far enough away from him." The kitchen timer dinged and Hope drained her glass.

"Dinner's ready, but I want you to finish your story." Chance hopped from his chair and headed back to the kitchen. "Want more wine?"

Maybe the whole damn bottle? "Sure. Can I help?" She got up and admired his backside in a pair of faded jeans.

"I got it but you can take a seat at the table." He set a steaming dish of baked goodness in the center on a trivet.

"Can I at least pour you more wine?" She set her now empty glass on the table and reached for the bottle.

"Absolutely." He brought over a tossed salad and garlic bread. As soon as Hope finished pouring, Chance pulled her chair out.

"Thanks. I guess it's been awhile since anyone besides my older brother did something nice for me," she said, sitting.

Not missing a beat, he picked up her plate and started to scoop ziti onto it. "You didn't finish about your ex." Then he set her plate in front of her. The dark blue sweater he wore made his eyes shimmer like the Caribbean Sea. "Did he not treat you well?"

She let out a half laugh, reaching for garlic bread then handing him the basket. "Not even close." She looked down at her food. Suddenly, the courage to look at Chance when she shared her past slipped away. "He was an abuser."

"He hit you?" There was no mistaking the change of tone in his voice. It had gone from happy go-lucky to lethal.

"Hit, humiliated, you name it, and he did it almost daily. He was a pro at making sure he left no marks where anyone might see."

A gray storm passed through his eyes. "How long were you with him?"

She drank more wine. "Three years."

"Jesus, Hope. Why so long? Did he threaten you or your family?"

"He left me an empty shell. I had no self esteem left by the time he was done with me." Some days she wondered if she really had recovered. His words had always hurt more than his hands. Now, sitting across from the first man since she had left David, she had to remind herself that Hope Sinclair was a survivor. She deserved happiness and would have it.

"Damn, I'm sorry. No woman should be treated like that. Not ever."

She picked at her dinner, determined not to let old memories ruin the evening. "I finally came to my senses, and when my brother found out... Well, he wanted to kill David but I got him settled down when I promised to leave everything behind and move. Eric helped get me set up here. He takes care of my finances, has for years, and I have a nice nest egg."

Chance shook his head, danger danced in his eyes. "If you were my sister, no fucking way would your ex still be breathing."

Hope finally took a bite of food, believing Chance would indeed carry out that threat to protect his sibling. She had been hard pressed to contain her own brother and even today wasn't sure Eric hadn't confronted David. It was all in the past, but sometimes she looked over her shoulder, fear nipping at her heels.

"This is really good. Do you cook for the guys?"

"Sometimes. Derrick's been doing most of the cooking since he got here."

"Speaking of, I got an invite to the wedding. A January wedding, it should be a good time." Hope loved weddings and couldn't be happier for the couple who seemed so much in love.

"Yeah, I still can't believe they are getting married and Kadin seems okay with it," Chance laughed.

"I did hear that he could be a bit overbearing with his sisters." She stabbed at her salad.

"A bit? I'm sure both Halee and Bella would have a lot to say on that matter."

Hope was positive they did, but one thing was certain, she was grateful for her own brother.

"This might be a strange request, but what if we went together? To the wedding?" Chance asked. "Unless of course you already have someone to go with," he rushed.

She stared across the table at him. "As in a date or as friends?" She hated to ask but needed to be clear. There was a big difference between the two.

"I would like to think as both."

Well, now that was an interesting reply.

———

Chance packed some of the leftover baked ziti into a plastic container while Hope loaded the dishwasher. He'd tried to get her to take a glass of wine and sit by the fire while he cleaned up, but she would have none of it so he let her help. He liked Hope. It was different talking to her outside the diner and getting to know her better. What he didn't like was knowing another man had laid his hands on her. Had bruised her skin and her soul. Those thoughts made the dragon inside him want to come out and play.

Rough.

Really, really, rough.

It had taken more willpower than he'd used in a long time to shove his anger deep so he didn't scare Hope. He never understood how a man could do violent things against the very female he should be protecting.

"So," Hope's voice cut into his dark thoughts, forcing him to focus on her. "I hope you don't mind if I say this, but I find it fascinating that you're a shifter."

He usually didn't talk about what he was while on a date, but this wasn't like most dates he went on. Those were for one reason only, and he and the female he was with usually skipped dinner and went straight for dessert. By now, they would be fucking their brains out. Hope was definitely sexy, and if he were scouring the bar, he would pick her up in a hot second. But she wasn't some woman he had smooth talked into his bed. She was Hope Sinclair. A woman who had packed up her life and ran for cover. One who served him breakfast on occasion and always had a smile to offer. The first woman since Mia that made him pause and wish he had more. The guys would laugh if he admitted he envied Derrick Taylor and the fact Derrick was settling down.

"You're not afraid?"

She took a sip from her glass. "Why would I be afraid?"

He shrugged. "Some people are."

She pulled her bottom lip through her teeth, and he stifled a groan. She wasn't supposed to tempt him, yet she had been a temptation since he first laid eyes on her. Chance should be busy flirting with one of the local blue hairs and making them feel twenty years younger then send them home with a kiss on the cheek. Next year, when the bachelor auction came up they would bid again. Between the small group of them, each one had taken turns winning a night with him since the auction had started several years ago. Again, he recalled Derrick's words from a few months back.

"That girl has the hots for you."

Shit, was Hope looking for a one-night stand or did she want more? He sure as hell didn't want to make Hope a one-time thing. One rule he followed was he fucked no one from his community. He always went to the city for his fun. It made for a cleaner break.

"There's not much information out there about you guys. I guess I don't even understand where you came from."

He handed her a towel. "Lets refill our glasses. I can tell you whatever you want while we digest and make room for the awesome dessert you brought." He went ahead and filled their glasses and carried them into the living room. This time he placed both on the same side of the coffee table and waited for her to sit before he plopped down next to her.

You're a fucking idiot. You should be sitting across the room. Not closer!

He liked how she smelled. A mixture of lemon zest and spring rain. Intoxicating, and something inside him shifted. Wanted to draw her to him but he fought the urge. Instead, he reminded himself she was out of his reach. Too good for someone like him. His dragon was quick to disagree, however.

"My ancestors come from Ireland. The story about how we came into existence has been passed down for generations."

Her eyes widened and she leaned back into the couch, wine glass in hand.

"Thousands of years ago, in a remote area called the Wicklow Mountains, lived a dragon. She was the last of her kind, all the others had died but no one knows why or how. It's said that Ophi was a very strong dragon. A female with the most powerful magic among her kind. Might explain why she had outlived the rest of them."

He took a sip of wine. "Anyway, Ophi knew if she didn't do something, when she perished her species would be gone forever. So she used her magic and turned herself into a human. While she lived as a human female, she took many husbands and bore lots of children. Because her magic was so powerful, her children were able to shift into a dragon at will."

Hope let out a small gasp. "Wow, I love that story. You're part of something so incredible. So precious. It sounds like Ophi was a strong, determined woman. It's a shame she's not still alive, I would have loved to meet her."

Chance had never thought much about his past, but Hope saw it as something wonderful. Now that she had said it, well...so did he. He would bet anything Hope was as strong a female as Ophi. Both women had fought for survival and won. Hope would be a fierce protector of her children one day. Of that he was certain.

"So, do you have magic? I-I mean besides being able to shift.

What does it feel like to change? What do you look like?" She bit her lip. "Damn, I'm sorry. I shouldn't ask so many questions."

He couldn't help but let out a laugh. She was simply too adorable and made him comfortable and willing to share the demons in his closet.

5

H ope was an idiot.

Since Chance had sat down next to her, all she could do was stutter and ask stupid questions. There was no helping it though, his body heat seeped into her even from a distance. Then there was his scent that reminded her of the outdoors. Woodsy, fresh, and sexy as hell. All she wanted to do was grab him by the shirt, jerk him close, and kiss him. It was a shame she didn't have the courage.

"I'm not laughing at you, but I like your enthusiasm. I once knew a woman who was frightened of what I am."

Hope didn't understand how that was possible, but the pain that passed through his eyes—as brief as it was—told her the woman was someone he had cared for a great deal.

"You don't frighten me. The opposite actually. I would love to see you shift some time."

He only smiled. "Each of us are able to shift into what is called our primary dragon. That dragon is a particular size and color and brings us the most power. However, we can change into any size and color dragon. It comes in handy at times if we need to fit into tight places. As far as magic, we all have different abilities. Usually the older we are, the stronger our powers and the more magic we hold.

There are some that have the ability to keep a person's soul from leaving their body."

"Why would you do that?" She leaned closer. Damn, maybe she was getting braver.

"It can be handy in our line of work. I have a friend, who is a halfling, inherited that trait from her father. She works as a paramedic and once, after a bad car accident, she kept a mother alive long enough to deliver her unborn child."

"Oh my God! Can you do that?" Hope didn't need to work in the medical field to understand how handy that would be.

"No. Though I can see inside someone and find any injuries. I see anything that has been wrong with them as well as any current issues, including mental. I can't heal them, but it can be helpful to the medical team."

Panic crawled up Hope's spine. Did Chance see the mended breaks or her emotional breakdown?

"Hope, you okay? You look like you've seen a ghost."

She thought she was okay with him knowing her past, but having him *see* it was something all together different. "I'm fine."

He studied her. "I can only see inside someone if they allow me to. I don't go around invading a person's privacy. Unless of course they are knocked out and in distress. I then have to assume they would consent to medical attention."

"Oh. Well that makes perfect sense." Whew, that was a close call. She glanced at the time. "Are you ready for dessert?"

"Sure, but I did promise you a tour of the house. Would you still like to see it?"

"Yes, if you don't mind." Truth be told, she was dying to see how he lived. From what she'd seen so far, he was into the rustic woodsy feel. She liked it very much.

He rose and offered his hand. She slipped her fingers across his palm and swore an electric current sizzled over her flesh. Her heart beat faster as he helped her to her feet, and briefly, their gazes met. When he released his grip, she was left with nothing more than a cold, empty feeling. Then that delectable mouth of his curled into a smile and warmed her to her toes.

"This way." He led her out of the living room, across honey colored floors, and she suddenly realized they were warm.

"Are the floors heated?"

"Yeah. Winters can be brutal and long up here." He glanced at her. "Course, you've been here long enough to know that."

"Boy have I. Those really cold, snowy nights, Harley and I curl up under a fuzzy blanket and watch TV."

"Harley?"

"My maltipoo. I got him from the shelter shortly after I moved here. He was just a pup and had been left by his owners so I took him home." She looked around. "Do you have any pets?"

"No, but I love dogs. Hard to have one though when I live alone and work twenty-four hours away from home."

"If it were not for Harley, there would be a lot of lonely nights." Oh, my God! She had not just said that to him. *Dumb, dumb, dumb, Hope. Way to look desperate.*

He ignored her comment and showed her the entertainment room. "The guys like to come over and play pool or watch the game." There was no missing the giant flat screen on the wall with several cozy recliners positioned for the best viewing pleasure. They walked past a bar on one side of the room.

"This is amazing."

"The best is yet to come." He pushed open a door and they entered a large open room. One side was walled with windows framing the lake and snow covered pines. Across from the expanse of glass sat several lounge chairs and tables. Opposite where they stood, a massive stone fireplace waited in silence to warm the room. But what took her breath was what all of these items surrounded.

"Holy shit!" She blinked, half expecting the room to change but it didn't. The large oval swimming pool still shimmered like a mirror in the middle of the room, reflecting the full moon that shone in from outside. Her gaze was drawn upward to the high peaked ceiling.

Thick heavy timbers hid lights that cast a golden glow across the entire room.

"This is my favorite room in the house. I love to swim and the pool is heated, making it comfortable for anyone."

She glanced over at him. "For anyone?"

"Shifters prefer the cold over heat. I'll swim in the lake up until it freezes."

She shivered at the mere thought of the current water temperature outside. The lakes in the Kirkwood area were normally frozen by early to mid-November, but this year had been warmer, and the water wasn't completely frozen over on many of the bigger lakes.

"I can't even begin to imagine." Another shiver crawled up her spine. "This, though, looks divine."

"I didn't even think to tell you to bring a swim suit. Maybe next time you come over."

Hope tried to slow her rapidly beating heart. He expected her to come over again? Hell yes and how soon?

———

Chance had taken Hope through the rest of the house. When they had gone to the upper level and he had shown her his room, his naughty side immediately wanted to shove her onto the bed and find out what she looked like beneath those clothes. However, he had behaved and now they were back in the kitchen.

"Shall we have dessert?"

"Absolutely," Hope said.

Chance grabbed plates and forks along with some napkins then handed her a knife, as well as something to lift the slices off the platter. Hope cut two pieces of the chocolate raspberry ganache cake, placed them on the plates, and then handed him a piece.

"That looks sinful," he said.

"Oh, it is. Wait until you taste it." She watched him while he took his first bite.

"Wow, that's really good."

She laughed and Chance realized for the first time since Mia, he was having fun with someone of the opposite sex without actually having sex. Dare he even contemplate the thought that raced through his head? Obviously, Hope wanted something from him. He had made sure to be sensitive to her from the time she'd walked in the door. Noting when her heart rate increased. The way her pupils dilated when she looked at him. Maybe she didn't want anything more than a casual relationship. They both stood at the counter eating cake when he finally decided to speak up.

"I've had a really good time with you tonight."

She set down her fork and licked her lips. "Me too. Thanks for dinner. It's been nice hanging out with you."

Her heart sped up again so he leaned closer.

"You have chocolate on your mouth. Let me help you with that." He was either going to get shoved away or not, but Chance was a risk taker. He gently kissed the corner of her mouth, tasting chocolate mixed with Hope. It was hard to separate the two, and when he leaned back, he wanted to taste more of her.

She swallowed "Y-you... Shit."

"I would apologize but I'm not sorry. Are you?" He sure as hell wanted to do it again.

"Only sorry that you stopped. I like you, Chance. I figured by now you knew that."

He either finished what he started or stop this train now before it derailed. He leaned closer. Took in her zesty, fresh rain scent and placed his mouth on hers. At first he simply peppered her lips with soft kisses. She moaned. He laid one hand on her hip and the other he slid into her hair.

Her silky locks slipped between his fingers and he backed her into the counter, careful to still keep distance between them. He wasn't ready to let her feel the erection that pressed against his zipper. Hope wasn't one of his conquests.

She was softness. Everything that was warm and good in the world and he would not take advantage of that. This was simply a kiss. An exploration of a beautiful woman and if there was ever any more to it than that, then he would cross that bridge then. This was him, simply sating his curiosity.

Her lips parted and her tongue darted out to meet his in a sensual dance. Heated desire ripped through him and his dragon stirred again.

Odd.

Chance's dragon never tried to surface with a woman. Apparently, his beast liked Hope.

He deepened the kiss and swore the dragon inside him rumbled with pleasure, and as much as he wanted more, he broke away. Locked on her gaze before he moved down to her swollen lips, red from his kiss. For the first time in his long life, he was at a loss as what to do or say next. This took him off guard. Chance was always in control.

He took a step back and shoved his hands in his pockets to keep them locked at his side.

"You're a good kisser," she whispered. Thank God it was her who broke the silence because he was certain he would have said something utterly ridiculous.

"You're pretty good yourself." Okay, that was fucking lame. Where was the smooth talking Chance? Out of service apparently.

She offered a smile. "I should probably go. Harley will need to go out soon."

Whew. Her leaving was good. Right? Yeah, because maybe his fucking dick would finally deflate.

"Let me grab your stuff." He headed for the fridge to get her leftovers.

"You keep the cake. If it comes to my house, my hips will only get wider," she joked.

"You have perfect hips, but are you sure you don't want a piece to take?" He really wanted to say her hips were perfect for gripping while he slid in and out of her, but he did have some sense.

"No. You can drop the platter off next time you're in town. No hurry."

"Okay. Thanks." He walked her to the door and helped her get her coat on then walked her outside to her vehicle. After she was buckled in, he leaned in and gave her a quick kiss on the lips.

"Can I call you?"

"I'd love that."

"Be careful driving home. Text me so I know you made it."

She gave a nod. "I will and thanks again." She put her SUV in drive and drove around the half circle until she was headed down the lane. He watched for as long as he could then headed back inside. Wondering what the hell had happened to the Chance who would have seduced Hope straight into his bed.

———

Hope had been floating on a cloud for the past week. Chance had kissed her and she scarcely believed it. Better yet, he'd called as promised and they had chatted for an hour and even met for dinner. Twice. Thanksgiving was at the end of the week, and Chance had to work the holiday so she wouldn't be seeing him again until after Thanksgiving. It was just as well. Eric, Hope's brother, was coming for a short visit. He would be arriving tonight and planned to spend a couple of days so he could get back to his wife and kids before Thanksgiving.

Harley barked, his entire butt wagging like a crazy pup. She laughed. "You know what this is, don't you?" She held up a small Christmas stocking with his name stitched on the front. The dog barked again.

"It's not time yet, soon though you silly boy." Hope had begun digging out her decorations, and when Eric arrived, he was going to help her decorate. Everything except the tree. She planned to go and cut a real one after Thanksgiving. She loved the scent of a fresh cut tree in her small house.

Her phone dinged and she set down the box, swiping the phone off the table. A text from Eric.

Hey sis, just landed. I need to grab my rental and should be there shortly.

Hope texted back. Can't wait to see you!

She set her phone back on the table and headed for the kitchen. She was sticking to their sibling tradition of eating pizza while they pulled out decorations. They would reminisce as they went through every box and found treasures from their childhood. Hope and Eric had lost their parents when Hope was eighteen and Eric twenty-three. Their mom and dad had taken a trip to Lake George for their anniversary, and on the way back, the small plane developed engine trouble. As experienced as the pilot had been, he hadn't been able to safely land. All three occupants were killed on impact. Hope would never forget the call that had come nearly twenty-two years ago. She still missed them both terribly, and had it not been for Eric, she wasn't sure she would have come out the other side. Her brother moved her to the city with him and helped her start a new life.

Shoving painful memories aside, she pulled the pizza from the fridge and set it on the counter to come to room temperature. She loved the small pizza shop that made fresh, ready to bake pies to take home and pop in the oven. Next, she opened the wine and set the bottle on the table. By the time she pulled out napkins, plates, and started the oven, her doorbell was ringing. Hope raced to the front door and flung it open.

Eric grinned at her from the front porch. "Hey, Sis. I got here a little faster than expected." He spread his arms and she flew into them. His hug was comfort, strength, and sibling love all rolled into one.

"I've missed you," she whispered.

"Me too." He gave a squeeze. "Now invite me in, it's damn cold out here."

She released him and stepped aside. Eric let the pack slide down his shoulder as he entered the house. Once inside, he dropped the backpack and scooped up a crazy Harley, who proceeded to lick him senseless.

"Okay, buddy. I love you too." Eric carried the dog into the living room and plopped him on the carpet.

"I'm ready to put the pizza in the oven." Hope walked into the small kitchen, pulled open the oven door, and shoved their dinner inside. "Wine?" she asked setting the timer.

"Got beer?" Eric lifted the bottle and poured one glass.

"In the fridge. Want a glass?"

He opened the fridge and pulled out a bottle and twisted off the cap. "Nope, straight from the bottle is fine." He took a swig then wiped his mouth. "So, how are things going here?" He handed her the wine glass.

"Great." She couldn't stop the smile that tugged at her mouth.

"Sis? What's going on to cause such a grin?" Eric took a seat on the couch and looked at her, expecting an answer.

"Remember the guy I told you about?" She sat next to him and curled her legs under her.

"Yeah, he's a firefighter you were bidding on at some bachelor auction."

"That's the one. Well, I won the bid and had my date."

He swigged his beer. "How'd that turn out for you?"

"Awesome. We've already been on a couple of dates."

"Is he a good guy?"

"He's nothing like David." She ran her finger around the rim of her glass. "I told him about my past."

"How'd he react?"

"He thought it was wrong, of course."

Eric took another swig of beer. "Sis, you should know David's out of prison. Happened last week."

She pulled in a deep breath. "I knew his release was coming up soon." She shrugged it off. "He's not going to bother with me now that I'm nowhere to be found." David had been sent to prison after the last time he had tried to strangle her. Eric had found the best attorney in the city, and with the documented evidence of his abuse, along with the marks on her neck and the doctor's testimony, they had managed to get David confined for three years.

The timer buzzed and Hope stood. "Pizza's done." Just in time, because she didn't want to think about or discuss David any longer.

6

Hope blew out the last candle then looked down at her dog. "Come on, Harley. Time for bed." It had been a long day and she was beat. Hope had volunteered to serve turkey dinner at the local shelter. The crowd had been bigger than in previous years after the mill fire left so many with no income. It had been rewarding work though, and everyone had a great time coming together. She stifled a yawn as she headed down the hall to her room. After washing her face and brushing her teeth, she donned flannel pajamas and crawled into bed. Harley tucked in next to her. Moments later, she drifted into a deep sleep.

Something tickled her nose and burned the back of her throat. Hope inhaled and went into a coughing fit. Opening her eyes, she realized she wasn't dreaming.

She smelled smoke.

"Dear"—cough—"God." Hope pushed herself off the bed and rolled onto the floor. In the darkness, glass shattered and she briefly wondered why the smoke detectors were not going off. After feeling her way to the door, she spotted flames at the end of the hall. Thinking quickly, she slammed her bedroom door shut. There was no way she was getting out through the front of the house. Managing to fight her way back to the window, she covered her mouth and nose with her pajama top. Her knee came down on something hard, causing her to cry out. Reaching for the object, she realized it was her cell phone. At least some luck was on her side.

Time came to a screeching halt as she fumbled with the window locks, but somehow finally managed to twist them and shove the window open. With her heart racing, she cursed the old house with the double panes. No matter how she fought to remain calm, she still had to get the storm open.

Between fits of coughing and not being able to see past the darkness and the tears in her eyes, she managed to win the battle with the storm and pushed it up. Shoving her head outside, cold air slapped her skin, and she hacked so hard she swore her ribs bruised.

"Hope!"

"Dan?" Her voice was a mere squeak, but she thought her neighbor called out to her.

"You're going to have to climb out the window. The entire front of your house is on fire!"

"I c-can't. Harley's still in here somewhere." God, she prayed he hadn't left the room.

"Hope, you have to get out and let the firefighters find the dog. Now, get moving! I'll help you."

Only because the sirens blared in the distance, and she knew she was no good to anyone dead did she follow Dan's advice and climb out the window. Thankfully, her house was a raised ranch and her window not far from the ground. Dan grabbed her legs and caught her in his arms.

"Harley," she sobbed.

Dan trudged through the snow, his wife came running with a blanket and threw it around Hope. "Snuggle into this. The fire department has arrived," Dan's wife said.

Even with the blanket, Hope was unable to stop shaking but not from the cold. She didn't even notice. Her only thought was on the small furry creature inside she had promised to care for. Vowed the day she adopted him to never let him down.

She was a complete and utter failure.

When Dan carried her to the firefighters, she noticed **O'Connell** written on the back of one of the coats.

Chance.

He rushed to her. "Hope. Are you okay?" There was no mistaking the tremor in his voice.

"Harley. Please find him." She broke into an uncontrollable sob. "You have to save him." She had no idea what she would do if Harley didn't make it out alive.

———

When the alarm roused Chance from a deep sleep, he'd gone on autopilot as always when he was on duty. It was only while he geared up that his brain finally engaged and caught the address of the call.

His heart sank into the pit of his stomach when he realized Hope's house was on fire.

Neighbors who called 911 were certain the homeowner was still inside. So when Chance jumped into the engine, Reese turned.

"I'm sure she's fine."

Never, in all of his years of service, had he wanted to throw up. Instead, he searched for calm as Derrick touched his shoulder.

"You got this."

Chance gave a nod. He'd fake his fucking way through this if necessary, but he'd do his damn job.

When Reese finally drove them out of the station, time slowed to a crawl. The four minutes it took for them to get to Market Street was an eternity. When they were finally into position, the shifter inside Chance rippled under the surface, threatening to break free and do what would require special equipment and training in his human form. His dragon, however, needed none of that to enter a burning structure and save a life. A life he prayed hadn't been snuffed out.

Fuck, he despised rules. The rules of his people that forbade him to shift in front of any human or face a severe penalty. It was an outdated law but change took time. Too damn much of it. In the meantime, those around him suffered and he had to question if this was a test for him. While he and Hope had only recently started dating, he had been pining for her since the day he'd walked into the diner and she'd served him a smile. He only wished he had asked her out much sooner.

When Chance pushed open his door, he prayed he would still get to spend a lot more time with Hope. Already he'd learned she had been a survivor once, but could she do it again? When his boots hit the snow-covered ground, he spotted a man carrying a woman from around the back of the house, and his heart skipped several beats.

"Hope?" he called as he ran to them.

"Harley. Please find Harley." She began to sob. "You have to save him."

Relief had his muscles relaxing and his mind back on the job, but her pleas to save her precious pooch had him promising her anything. "Does he have a favorite spot?"

"He sleeps with me, but he wasn't there when I woke up."

"How many bedrooms do you have and where is yours located?"

"Three——"

"Hers is back left corner," the neighbor cut Hope off.

"Okay, now let the paramedics check you, and I'll try to locate Harley." He started to turn when she reached for him.

"I closed the bedroom door. I hope that was the right thing to do."

"It was the perfect thing to do." If the dog had gone under the bed, closing the door might just save his life. He searched for and found Gaelen.

"Captain, there's a dog inside, other than that she lives alone." Chance studied the fire that had shattered the front windows and was followed by thick black smoke. An acrid stench filled the air.

Gaelen gave a nod. "I already have Doyle rigging for hydro ventilation. The living room and kitchen appear to be involved. We'll use hydroventing here in the front. You take Taylor and go to the back. There's a sliding glass door off the kitchen. Once things cool down, I'll give the command to go in. Hopefully you'll encounter the dog."

While they spoke, Doyle had already rigged the Hydrovent, a special suppression and ventilation nozzle used to both cool the interior and assist with venting. It was placed in the front window, and within seconds, black smoke turned white and was pulled outside while the inside of the house cooled from the suppression nozzle.

A damn handy tool that had been invented by a firefighter then tweaked by his son.

"Got it." Chance headed toward the group of men pulling in line. "Taylor?" he shouted.

"Yeah?" Derrick straightened from the hose he was dragging.

"You're with me. We're going to the back, and we got a small dog inside guys so keep alert." Chance clicked on his helmet light then picked up the hose. He and Derrick trudged through several inches of snow, pulling line as they went until they reached the deck on the back of the house. Dropping the line, both he and his partner masked up then checked the patio door.

Unlocked.

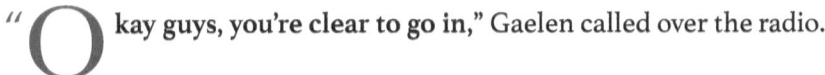

"Okay guys, you're clear to go in," Gaelen called over the radio.

"Copy," Chance replied. With Derrick on the nozzle, Chance followed, pulling hose behind him. They entered through the kitchen where the flames claimed a wall that separated the kitchen from the living room. Ash and Devin charged through the front door and made an attack from the other side. From first assessment, the fire already took out most of the living room, but the Hydrovent was doing what it had been designed to. Knock down the worst so they could attack from inside. Hopefully, the quick cooling and ventilation saved the dog because Chance didn't want to present Hope with her deceased pup.

Derrick was quick to knock down the remaining flames in the kitchen, and it appeared the worst was in the living room. Likely where the fire had started. Torin was pulling ceiling to make sure it hadn't spread into the attic. So far, the heaviest damage was located in front of the window.

"I'll help you look for the dog while we check the rest of the house." Derrick shut down his nozzle.

"Let's head down the hall." Even though the smoke was clearing, it was still heavy so Chance dropped to his knees and began to crawl, sweeping his arms out in front of him to feel for anything. Visibility was still shitty at best, and he didn't want to miss a small furry creature. When he came to a doorjamb, he reached and beat his gloved fist on the floor.

"Taylor, I got tile floor here."

"Copy. Look clear?"

"I don't see any fire." It was a good sign that hopefully the fire had been contained to the kitchen and living room. He crawled forward a few more feet when he met something solid. Feeling around, he discovered it was a door and rose up to his knees. "I think we hit the master." He twisted the knob and shoved the door open. The room was surprisingly clear and he pushed to his feet, able to see to walk in.

"There's a room over here," Derrick called out. "I'm going to clear it."

"Okay." If not for the mask, Chance's shifter senses would be able to scent the dog. Instead, he dropped back to his knees and shined his light under the bed. At first he saw nothing except a few boxes, and then he spotted something out of place. Something soft against the hard lines of cardboard. He flattened himself to the floor and stretched his arm as far as he could.

"Damn it. Harley?" The dog was only fingertips away, yet he might as well have been on the other side of the room. In frustration, Chance hopped back up and moved to the other side of the bed. When he dropped back down, he reached in and this time was able to grab the dog and pull him out. With the small pup cradled against him, he noted Harley was alive but in distress.

"I gotcha little one." He stormed from the room. "Taylor, I got the dog."

"Awesome. All is clear on this side of the house. No evidence of fire," Derrick replied.

With the hall now clearer than before, the men made their way on foot back to the living room where nothing more than a few cinders still burned. Chance headed for the steps down to the front door and, once outside, raced to the ambulance where Hope sat inside with a couple of blankets wrapped around her.

"Harley!" The devastated expression on her face gutted him.

"Halee?" Chance shouted through his mask as he reached into the cabinet for the pet oxygen kit.

"On it," she replied.

Chance pulled a small mask from the kit and fitted it over the dog's muzzle while Halee grabbed tubing and connected it to oxygen. Hope ran her hand over Harley and whispered soft words to him.

Chance finally took a moment to pull his mask off. "Hope, how are you doing?" He sent a questioning glance toward Halee, who gave him a nod.

"I'm fine. Is he going to be okay?"

The sound of her hoarse voice pained him.

"He should come around in a few minutes, but he'll need to get checked by the vet." Halee placed a reassuring hand on Hope's shoulder.

"I can call him now." Chance noticed Halee clutched a cell phone in her hand.

He gave Halee a nod. "Why don't you do that? I'll go in and retrieve some clothes for you." His attention was back on Hope. "Anything else you might need?"

She looked up at him. Tears still filled her eyes. "I... I'm not sure. My purse was in the living room with all my cash and credit cards. I guess I should call my brother and see if he can book me a hotel room." She looked back at her pup, who was coming round. "Well Harley, looks like we're going to have to make some adjustments, but at least we are alive."

"Hope, you and Harley will come stay with me." Chance didn't even need to think about it.

She started to hesitate.

"*No* is not an option." Then he walked away to help his team clean up and get Hope some of her things.

7

Hope reeled over the fact her house was still smoldering and from the looks of it, nearly destroyed. Kadin, the station's chief, strode toward her.

"The living room is almost completely gone and the kitchen took a beating. From the looks of it, the fire started by the front window. Were you burning candles?"

"I was but blew them out before I went to bed."

He seemed to contemplate for a moment. "Its possible they reignited."

"My smoke detectors didn't go off either. I don't know why they didn't go off." Tears threatened again so she stroked the pup in her lap. Dr. Vitner should be along any minute. The vet had promised to come and pick the dog up and take him in for examination.

"Did you change the batteries?"

"Yes, only last month and tested the alarms."

Kadin scratched his jaw. "Well, there will be an investigation. Maybe we can come up with some answers."

Chance approached, a bag in his hand. "I grabbed what I thought you might need for a few days." He faced Kadin. "She's going to my house. Any chance you can drop her off?"

"Sure. Throw those in my truck."

"Umm, excuse me." Everyone stopped to look at her. "Don't I get a say in this?"

"Look Hope, you've been through a lot tonight. I have plenty of room. Hell, I have three guest rooms, you can pick which one you want."

"I don't want to put you out." It was difficult to look at him without a tingle sliding over her skin. Even dressed in his turnout gear and smudges of soot across his cheek, the man was sex walking. Christ, how could she even think about that at a time like this? But everything about Chance made her mind and body feel things that confused the hell out of her. One glance from those pools of blue undid her.

"I'll be off in a few hours. Let me help you out, Hope."

It was the softness in his voice that had her giving in. "Okay. Thank you."

He gave a satisfied nod then walked off with her bag in hand. Out of the darkness, Dr. Vitner finally came forward.

"Hope, are you hurt?" he asked. She'd always liked the doctor and Harley loved him, which made handing her baby over much easier.

"Doctor Vitner, I'm fine. I'm hoping you'll tell me that Harley is as well."

The man offered his usual warm smile then picked up a tail-wagging Harley. "Well, his attitude is a good sign." By now, the dog was licking his face.

"We gave him oxygen as he was pretty lethargic when the firefighter brought him out," Halee offered. "He came around fairly quick."

"Thanks." He brought his attention back to Hope. "I'll check him over and clean him up. Can I call your cell?"

"Yes. Please call me as soon as you know how he's doing."

He gave a nod then walked away with the only family she had with her tucked to his chest. The tears burned her eyes again, and she had to shove them away.

"Hope, let me drive you to Chance's. I have an extra key and can help you get settled in." Kadin held out a coat—her coat—that she donned and tried not to gag at the smell now embedded into the fabric. Her life had changed in a matter of seconds, but she forced herself to remember that both she and Harley were alive. The house could be repaired and possessions replaced.

C hance finally finished scrubbing the night's soot off his skin only an hour before his shift ended. Kadin had taken Hope to Chance's and reported back that she was safely tucked inside. Chance texted her only minutes ago to learn that Dr. Vitner had already given Harley the all clear on his health but wanted to keep the pup for grooming. He'd promised that the dog could be picked up later this afternoon.

"How you doing?" Reese stepped to his locker and started pulling out his street clothes.

"Me? I'm fine, why wouldn't I be?"

Reese laughed. "Don't think you can pull that shit on me. A guy doesn't offer his home to just anyone. Apparently, that woman has already gotten under your thick skin." Reese's forehead wrinkled. "Unless you're thinking to get lucky? I can't see Hope being the kind of gal who would have slept with you yet."

"Maybe I'm being a nice guy."

Reese laughed so hard he had actual tears leaking from the corner of his eyes.

"Fuck you, asshole." That comment only caused Reese to roar louder and slap his thigh. Several minutes later, his so-called friend regained his composure.

"Sorry dude, but I think Mr. One-and-Done has finally found someone who has garnered his interest."

Chance sat on the bench. "Is that a bad thing?"

Reese took a seat next to him. "Nah. Aren't you always telling me it's time to move on? Hasn't it been long enough since Mia?"

"I guess I've been thinking lately that I might be ready." He shrugged. "Hope... Well... Fuck, she caught my attention from day one, and I don't mean just for sex."

"It's about time you admitted you have a thing for her."

He gave Reese the stink eye. "What the hell?"

Reese stood and pulled on a clean shirt. "You really think none of us noticed how you looked at her? Idiot, even Derrick noticed and he's the new guy."

Chance stared at the floor. "Yet none of you harassed me about it?" There was definitely something wrong with that picture.

"Maybe because we didn't want to scare you off and hoped your dumb ass would come around. I like Hope. She's a wonderful gal. Besides, she's not Mia and already knows you have a scaly side." He laughed. "Time to go home."

Chance got up and finished changing and grabbed his cell. As he started to walk away, his phone dinged.

Hey, would it be ok if I borrowed a shirt? My stuff smells.

He typed back. Help yourself to anything you need.

Thanks.

He walked off with visions of Hope wearing nothing but his T-shirt. When he climbed in his truck twenty minutes later and headed down the road, he realized he couldn't get home fast enough after having received yet another text from Hope stating she had a surprise for him.

What. The. Hell?

His mind buzzed with all kinds of thoughts. Most of which

involved her naked beneath him, his fingers pressed into her hips as he thrust into her. Sent her on a spiraling fall into oblivion where she forgot everything but him and the pleasure he could bring her. When he stopped at the last light in town, snow began to fall. Forecasters were predicting an early storm that could possibly dump up to a foot of snow on the area. Storms were always trouble because power sometimes went out then people burned candles, used ovens, or any other means they had to stay warm. Travel was difficult and homes were destroyed.

Pressing the gas pedal, he drove out of town wishing the station's crew a quiet and uneventful shift. Chance was off for the next two days, and there was a lot to do. Thoughts of seducing Hope were sent into the back of his mind. Not that he didn't want the woman to warm his bed. Visions of her caused his dragon to stir. More than the beast usually did when Chance was busy seeking his next conquest. No, the last time his beast reacted to a female in this manner was Mia. Reese's words came back to him. While Mia had no idea what Chance really was, Hope seemed fascinated. Still, there was a big difference between knowing and actually *seeing* what Chance was. Inside him lurked a beast. One that held more power than any human could ever imagine. His people had the ability to do so many things to help, yet their hands were tied unless they broke the rules.

When he finally pulled into the driveway and parked in the garage, he had already decided he wasn't going to push things between him and Hope. She was in charge and would be the one dictating how fast things progressed between them. When he opened the door and walked into the kitchen, he found her standing at the stove. Spatula in one hand and the other on the handle of a skillet wearing only his tee, he quickly realized keeping his hands to himself was going to take everything he had.

———

Hope wanted to do something to thank Chance for everything he had done. Making breakfast seemed so small compared to saving Harley, but she knew there was nothing she could ever do to repay him for that. Offering her his home and even his own clothes was simply the cherry topping. She would cook for him morning, noon, and night if it made him happy.

"What's this?" How had he slipped in so quietly?

"Breakfast. It's not much but I wanted to thank you in some way for everything you've done."

He stepped closer and she swore his nostrils flared. Had it been her imagination?

"You didn't need to do this. You should be resting."

"I'm fine." She flipped the pancakes then reached into the other pan and turned the bacon. "Besides, I like to cook and never get to do much of it living by myself." She glanced over her shoulder. "You have had a long night and need a nourishing meal before bed."

Her cheeks heated at the mention of bed, and her mind immediately went to the visions of his naked chest that she still held in her head. Her lips recalled the taste of his kisses and how her entire body lit up every time he claimed her mouth. Hope pulled the pancakes from the pan and stacked them with the rest in the warm oven before she turned off the bacon and placed the pieces to drain on paper towels.

"You really didn't need to cook me breakfast." He brushed past her as he reached for a piece of bacon and took a bite. She couldn't stop staring at his mouth, which glistened from the grease. Before she could react, he touched the rest of the piece to her lips. She opened and he fed it to her. Time stopped while they both stared at each other. Her heart beat against her chest so loudly she was sure he heard it.

She licked her lips.

Deep blue eyes locked onto her mouth.

He cleared his throat. "I'll grab the syrup." Then he was gone and she was left wondering...

What. The. Hell?

Had she done something wrong? He certainly hadn't hesitated to kiss her the other night or on the couple of dates they had gone on. She would have laid money on him kissing her seconds ago. Suddenly she felt like a complete fool and turned to finish getting the food on the table when he snaked his arm around her waist. She closed her eyes and tried to push away all the desire that swept through her body.

"Hope," he whispered in her ear. "Don't think for a minute that I'm pushing you away. I want you."

"I-I'm confused." Her voice was barely audible.

"My reputation is no secret in this town, and frankly I made sure it wasn't. I never wanted any woman to get the wrong idea. It's also why I go to the city." He spun her to face him. "You are the first woman I've actually asked out since... Well, in a long time."

She sensed he left something unsaid.

"I'm giving you control of what happens between us. You decide how far and fast this goes."

It took her a moment to process his words and their meaning. "Is this because of my past or yours?"

"A little of both." He brushed a lock of hair from her cheek. "We better eat before it gets cold."

Hope gave a nod and pulled herself together. Moments later, they were both seated at the table quietly eating while she considered the gift the man across from her had just placed in her lap. Everyone joked that Chance O'Connell was a one-and-done man. He lived a carefree life, with a vow to never settle down. Certainly, a man most sane women would avoid like the plague. Yet here she was, literally in the dragon's lair.

8

It had been two weeks since Hope had moved in. Harley was now with them and Chance was taking a ribbing like nobody's business at the station. Just the other day, Reese had played the wedding march when Chance walked in, and Derrick asked if there was going to be a double wedding. Apparently, they were making up for their lack of harassment earlier.

Assholes.

Even Halee had gotten in on the action by making sure to leave bridal magazines lying everywhere. Chance might not have given it much thought, considering she was planning her own wedding except he found one on top of his pillow.

He was *so* going to pay them all back.

"Hey Chancy boy, did you mark her yet? I didn't notice your mark on her when she stopped by earlier." The six-foot-four, dark-skinned shifter rubbed his chin. A spark of mischief glistened in Ash's chocolate eyes. "She's a mighty fine looking woman, and I hear she can cook. I might mate her myself. Just think, our kids would be stunning." The entire firehouse roared with laughter. Chance knew Ash was giving him grief, but the thought of any other male touching Hope caused a spark to ignite in his fingertips.

Something crashed to the floor.

"Oh my God! Chance, did you just—?" Halee rushed forward, big brother Gaelen right behind her.

Chance looked at his hands and rolled his fingers into his palms.

"Son of a bitch," Gaelen exclaimed. "Can you do it again?"

"I have no idea." Were his hands actually shaking?

Halee touched his arm. "Chance, are you getting the gift?"

"I... Shit, I don't know. This is the first time it happened." He uncurled his fingers then balled his fists tight. His own body suddenly felt foreign to him and then a sinking thought hit him. Would he hurt Hope if he touched her? The very idea made him sick to his stomach.

Suddenly, the crowd parted and Kadin ate up the floor, heading toward them. "You have the magic of fire?"

"I don't know. This is the first time it's happened." How many times was he going to have to repeat it?

"I think Ash provoked him," Reese offered.

Kadin swung his gaze to Ash. "Explain."

The shifter lifted a heavy shoulder. "I only asked if he marked her then joked I'd be happy to do it for him."

Kadin studied Chance as if he were a specimen under a microscope. "Interesting. So, what I'm hearing is that when another male threatened your female, you created a spark."

"She is not my female," Chance growled.

"Seriously? She's living in your home." Kadin pointed it out as if Chance needed to be reminded. He was bombarded every second he was in the house by her scent. By her bright smile. Her home cooked meals and simply her company. The thing about it was he actually enjoyed having her there. Hadn't realized what he was missing all this time. In two weeks, he was seeing Hope with new eyes. She was the kindest person he'd ever met and one deserving so much better than him.

"Think of something that makes you angry." Kadin pulled him from his thoughts.

"What?"

"Anger. I'm guessing it's what sparked your... Well spark."

With a disgruntled sigh, Chance closed his eyes and pulled up the one image he knew would bring forth his ire. The scar he'd seen by accident on the back of Hope's left shoulder had him asking questions.

Hope exited the pool, water droplets trailed down her perfect body, and he nearly lost his willpower until she turned her back to him and he spotted the angry mark. "Hope, what's that scar from?"

She looked over her shoulder at him, sadness and pain filled her eyes. "It's nothing."

"That's not nothing." It was obvious she didn't want to talk about it.

She quickly threw a towel over her shoulders and ignored his comment. Against his better judgment, he rose from his chair and approached her, placing fingertips on her wrist. "He did that to you, am I right?"

She swallowed. "Yes. He was angry at me for lord only knows what and heated the top of a metal lighter then pinned me down and... Well the rest is obvious."

A dragon's fury boiled inside Chance as he pictured Hope crying out in pain. Both his hands began to tingle, and when he opened his eyes, everyone was staring at the melon-sized ball of fire floating in front of him.

"Son of a bitch," Kadin whispered.

"Please tell me you have control of that thing or we'll be putting our own station out." Reese took a step back.

"It's so beautiful." Leave it to Halee to think the inferno floating in front of them was something to be admired. Though, if Chance took a moment to really study it, it was a thing of beauty. Deep orange intertwined with yellow and red floated on a silent cushion of air, waiting for his command.

"Well congratulations, it's a boy. Or is it a girl? Either way you just birthed fire," Gaelen joked.

Chance concentrated on the flames. Imagined dousing them, smothering their fuel until they were no more, and slowly the ball shrunk until it was gone. Halee moved closer and touched his arm.

"Welcome to the exclusive club of rare shifters. I'm glad for the company." She pushed up on her toes and kissed his cheek before walking away. Halee was one of the only full-blooded female shifters in existence. And now, within a matter of seconds, Chance had joined his own rare club. Even in dragon form, none of them could conjure fire. It was an elusive entity to them. The last known dragon that held the magic of fire died long ago.

This was not a blessing but a curse. Another thing the elders would forbid if they found out, because the *tamolth*, the magic of fire, meant Chance now held power over the very thing they fought every day.

———

Hope had taken a long hot bath, soaking in the luxurious bubbles scented with lavender until she was nearly a prune. She'd then slathered lotion over her skin until it was silky soft. Chance would be home soon and a breakfast casserole baked in the oven. In the two weeks she had been a guest in his home, he had kept his word and was nothing short of a perfect gentleman.

She was about to end that.

Hope wanted the man who had kissed her that first night. Was desperate to feel the passion behind that very kiss. Curious to discover how that same frenzy would erupt in the bedroom. The thoughts that raced through her mind sent a shiver down her spine and moisture to her sex. Hope pulled on a new pair of jeans and a low cut, cream-colored sweater that clung to every curve. The new bra pushed her ample cleavage to a noticeable proportion. When she had been out to the insurance adjuster's office, she had stopped and picked up a few new things with the plan to make her intentions clear this morning. Chance was either going to take the bait or she was going to spell it out for him.

As she checked herself in the mirror, she decided if she wasn't sending a message of, *I need to get laid,* then she wasn't sure what would. If it boiled down to asking, then she was prepared to do that as well.

Harley ran from the room, an indication Chance was home. The dog was the only one who could hear the quiet shifter enter the house. Something that made her slightly nervous, but at least she had the Harley radar. Following the dog, she happened upon Chance bending down to greet the pooch as had become his habit. It seemed like the two had bonded, and she wondered if it had anything to do with the firefighter saving the dog's life. Might even be something as simple as animal instinct. She would have to ask Chance if there was anything between the shifters and other animals.

"Welcome home," she said.

He lifted his head and opened his mouth to speak then slammed it closed when he spotted her. "Good morning," he finally managed.

Had his pupils dilated? That would be a good sign of interest.

"Something smells good." He lifted his chin and sniffed the air.

"Breakfast casserole. I hope you're hungry."

"Starved."

She headed to the kitchen and he followed just as the oven timer went off. Hope pulled the dish from the oven and placed it on top of the stove. "It needs to sit for a few minutes before we can eat it." She started to set the table. "How was your shift?"

"Okay. Actually quiet, which was nice. For the most part."

She sensed something was off and stopped what she was doing to face him. "What's wrong?"

"Nothing. You look nice this morning."

Avoidance. Not happening since she had once been a pro at it. Hope rounded the table and moved in on him. Close enough to place her hand on his chest and feel his heat under the tips of her fingers. Heat that nearly made her shiver with desire. "Chance, I'm here if you want to talk about whatever is on your mind."

His gaze devoured her mouth. "You are temptation, Hope." Yet he never laid a hand on her. Only stood there as if he were afraid to touch her.

Well, she was done waiting. Hope leaned into him and placed a soft kiss on his lips. His scent, a wild woodsy breeze mingled with musk, intoxicated her. His arms slipped around her waist and tightened until their bodies melted together. There was no mistaking the hardness pressed against her belly.

He wanted her.

"I want you, Hope. Make no mistake about it," he murmured against her mouth.

She looked up into an ocean of blue speckled with flecks of emerald. "Your eyes, they're different." She had never seen the green before. The color was simply amazing and reminded her of a stormy sea.

"It seems you not only stoke my desire but that of the dragon. Does that frighten you?"

One would think it might frighten any female with a lick of common sense. Apparently, she had none when it came to this man. "No. Are you two different beings?"

"We're two yet we are also one if that makes sense. The beast's instincts, power, magic, they are all part of the man that I am. Just as my human nature, my ideals, and my very values are part of him when I shift."

She licked her lips. "Would you know me in your dragon form?"

"Most definitely. My humanity is what keeps the beast from becoming completely animalistic."

"Your world sounds like an amazing thing. You were blessed with a true gift."

———

Funny, at the moment he didn't feel like he was blessed with any gift other than the soft female pressed against him. The one who was clearly interested in having sex with him, so why did he hesitate? Maybe because he had just found out he was a fire dragon. Once the elders discovered this, they would be keeping a close eye on him. Would want to make sure he didn't do anything in front of the humans they felt would compromise the shifters. Would they try and force him to leave his home and go to Ireland?

"Chance?" Hope nuzzled his jaw. "Let's forget breakfast for now."

He grinned, able to forget his name if she kept nuzzling him. "What did you want to do instead?"

She tilted her head to look up at him, brows dipped. "Seriously?"

"I don't want to misunderstand your intentions." He bit back a chuckle when she took a step back, hands on her hips.

"Chance O'Connell, if you don't get this then you are daft." She grabbed the hem of her sweater and peeled the garment from her body, tossing it to the floor. A grin only the devil would offer curved her lips. "Understand yet?"

The woman stood in jeans and a red lacy bra that hardly covered a pair of perfect breasts. He tore his gaze away to move down to her narrow waist then end at her hips. He wanted to launch himself at her. Suckle those breasts until she begged him to take her. Yet he steeled himself, kept his feet planted firmly on the floor. "I must be daft, because I'm still not sure what you want. Perhaps you should give me another hint?"

"You're a beast."

"So I've been told."

She unbuttoned her jeans, pulled down the zipper then did a slow seductive wiggle out of them. When they fell to her ankles, she stepped free. "Any ideas in that thick skull of yours?"

Several. He was counting the ways he could have her yet enjoyed this little game. He scratched his head. "I'm afraid I'm still in need of another hint. I mean, I have to be positive as I would hate to guess wrong."

She scowled at him then a delicate brow arched, and he knew she was about to change the rules of this game. Reaching behind her, she unclasped her bra while holding it in place with one arm. Turning her back, she let the lace and satin fall to the floor. While he stood there struck dumb and staring at one fine ass, she walked away. Headed down the hall, yet all he could do was watch the way her hips swayed as she vanished around the corner.

"Fuck!" He toed off his boots and raced after her, ripping off his shirt as he went. When he hit the door to his private retreat, a pair of red panties hung on the handle beckoning surrender. The beast inside him growled as he lifted the fabric and caught Hope's arousal.

Mine.

His cock pressed so hard against his jeans he swore he was going to tear right through them.

He pushed open the door and stepped inside, his gaze immediately fell to the female in the pool. Water denied him the view of her perfect body but not for long. He tore at his jeans, somehow ridding himself of the annoyance. His erection jutted forward, searching for the female who had stirred such feral desire deep inside him.

"My, my. Looks like dragon boy finally got the hint." Hope laughed and swam to the other side of the pool.

"Dragon boy? I promise you I am no boy as you will soon find out." He dove in, water cooling his skin only slightly before he zeroed in on her. With a kick of his powerful legs, he pushed through the water until he reached her then surfaced. "Enough of the games. This is your last opportunity to end this. Tell me no, and I will walk away. Say yes, and I promise you more pleasure than you can handle."

9

A pair of strong arms pinned Hope to the side of the pool, while his gaze––green flecks swirling in a violent sea of blue––bore into her. His nostrils flared with every breath he pulled in, and Chance reminded her of a wild animal ready to strike. Yet, she wasn't afraid of him. Not even when she caught a glimpse of pearly points. Were those fangs that peeked out from his upper lip? She brought her fingertips to his mouth, and then they were gone.

"I would never hurt you. You know that, right?" he whispered.

Some might call her crazy because she was naked and at the mercy of a man who was half beast. She saw it in him. The dragon that wanted to surface. Even his scent had changed, it was wild, sensual, and it called to something inside her. Dared her to drop every barrier and bare her very soul to him. No, this was not a man who would ever say hurtful things to her. He would not raise a hand to strike her and would never direct his anger toward her. Yet, somehow she knew if they surrendered to each other, nothing would ever be the same between them again. There was a possibility she was wrong about what this was between them, and Hope would become another one of Chance's *one-and-done*. Or her gut was right and this would only serve to forge a bond between them. Everything in her screamed this man was the other half of her soul.

"Yes." No going back now.

He didn't hesitate when he claimed her mouth. His tongue plundering as he pressed his body and that beautiful full erection against her flesh. Heat tore through her and weakened her knees. She would have sunk deeper into the water if Chance didn't have hold of her.

She wiggled against him, desperate to have him inside her but his kiss only deepened. When he finally broke free, she drew in a deep breath, hoping to slow her racing heart.

It didn't help.

Chance kissed her neck. Ran his tongue along the column until he reached the sensitive flesh at the base where he suckled.

Her entire body became one glorious inferno of pent up passion, and she reached around, gripping his ass. The man was perfection sculpted from muscle and sinew. When he bent, sucking her nipple into the heat of his mouth, all she could do was surrender.

"Yes. More," she whispered.

He licked his way to her other breast. "Baby, I intend to worship every inch of your body." And then she was swept back into bliss as his tongue swirled around her nipple, hardening it to a painful peak. He lifted her, setting her gently on the edge of the pool, spreading her thighs. Hunger filled his eyes and she only craved him more.

With a tender caress, he ran his fingertips over the sensitive flesh between her thighs, causing her to hiss. His mouth drew closer until hot breath brushed across her, causing a shiver. Time stopped while she waited for that burst of pleasure to consume her.

He teased.

Tortured.

Until a swipe of his tongue caused her to arch, lift herself off the cool tile, trying with desperation to reach his mouth.

He pinned her down. His mouth twisted into a wicked grin. "Ah, baby. Do you want me to taste you?"

She struggled against his grip. "Yes. God, yes."

The words had barely left her mouth when his was on her and she began spiraling downward.

———

The sweet delectable taste of honey coated his tongue, and Chance had never wanted to devour a woman more. Sure, he always made certain the women he was with went away satisfied, but this was different. He wanted Hope's utter and complete surrender. Wanted her pleasure on his tongue then his cock. He wanted to mark her, claim her as his own.

What the ever-loving hell?

Since when did he want to claim a mate? He forced back the fangs that kept making an unwelcome appearance and instead concentrated on the delectable feast in front of him. She was on the threshold of orgasm, and he enjoyed holding her release back, knowing that when it finally came, she would be undone.

He ran his tongue along her inner thigh, kissing, eliciting small gasps of pleasure from the female at his mercy. He brushed his thumb along the naked swollen flesh at her center.

"You are such a tease." Her body trembled.

"Are you ready to come, baby?"

"P-please."

No more encouragement was needed. He flicked his tongue over her clit, inserted two fingers then watched her shudder into bliss. When her body finally relaxed, he nuzzled her thigh then lifted her back into the pool with him. His erection was now so painful he swore he would lose control the second he entered her.

"How are you doing, baby?" He led her to the shallows where he sat on a wide underwater ledge. Control was going to be hers, otherwise he was afraid he might hurt her. Become too rough because all he could think about was claiming her.

"I'm wonderful, but I hope we're not done yet," she purred.

"Not by a long shot." He still held her hand. "You're in charge, baby. Take what you want, how you want it."

She grinned as she positioned herself over him. The tip of his cock poised at her heated entrance. Her hands on his shoulders to help her balance, she sheathed herself over the head of his shaft, and it took every ounce of willpower he had not to thrust deep inside her. Instead, he cupped her breast, bent his head, and suckled a nipple.

She slid the rest of the way down his cock and settled on his lap.

They locked gazes. Hers was molten copper and he was certain his were a mixture of blue and green. The colors a combination of his human side and that of the dragon. Never had a female fit him more perfectly or felt more right.

She wiggled her hips, eliciting a moan from him before she raised then lowered herself. He dug his fingers into her hips and helped guide the pace. At first slow and steady, but as she moved closer to another orgasm, it became more frantic. Their flesh slapped together while ripples of water moved around them and then she cried out. The grip on his cock as she drenched him was more than he could bear. He lost himself as he was pulled into the depths of intense pleasure. When he finally opened his eyes and looked at her flushed cheeks, he knew with certainty this was far from finished.

———

Hope floated on a cushion of bliss as she finally pulled away from Chance. Sex with him had been mind blowing and she wanted more. So much more. It was like her desires would never be sated. Perhaps it was because he had given her full control of the situation and two fan-fucking-tastic orgasms. Both were something her ex had never given. Hope had waited for what seemed forever for this to happen. Had dreamed about the man in front of her on more nights than she cared to admit. She swore she had even dreamed of him before she had ever laid eyes on him. Maybe it was just her own messed up desire to have a man that actually cared about her. About her needs.

"Where have you gone, Hope?" He broke the silence.

"I'm still here." She offered a smile.

"You looked far away."

"You blew my mind, that's all." She laughed then swam away.

"Oh, I'm not done with you yet." He didn't make an effort to come after but watched her every move like a lethal predator as she climbed from the pool and grabbed a towel.

"Look, it's snowing." The expanse of glass framed enormous flakes floating on a gentle breeze. She wrapped the towel around her then padded across the heated tile to stand in front of the glass. Before she realized it, Chance was behind her. His arms locked around her waist and his mouth on her neck.

"We might get snowed in," he whispered.

"Whatever would we do?"

"I can think of something."

Her towel slipped to the floor, and suddenly he was leading her to a large faux fur rug in front of the window.

"If I could lead you outside and make love to you in the snow, I would. This will have to do." He pulled her to the rug, into his lap, and kissed her. Hungry, passionate, demanding, and she returned the kiss with the same heated frenzy. Before she knew what was happening, he had her on her back, the kiss deepening as he entered her. His mouth moved from her lips and blazed a trail of heat down her neck. Hope would swear she felt a scrape of a pointed tooth on her skin.

He rested his elbows on either side of her head and cupped her face. "You have the most beautiful eyes, and I want to look into them when you come for me."

There. There they were, she had not imagined him having fangs. While butterflies in her stomach fluttered, she traced a finger over his lip. "They are real," she whispered.

"Are you frightened?" He'd stopped moving.

She gripped his ass. His wonderful, glorious ass. "Not at all." Then to prove it she kissed him. Ran her tongue across a point, eliciting a moan from him and he began to thrust.

Hard.

Fast.

And she realized those sexy fangs were sensitive to her touch and naughty thoughts entered her mind. As she started a spiral toward climax, he broke the kiss and stared into her eyes while she totally shattered. His cock swelled further and his own release followed. It was then she noticed what looked like fire in his eyes. Surely it had to be her imagination. After an earth-shattering orgasm, she was likely to see many things, though flames wasn't one she expected.

He buried his head in her neck and planted a soft kiss. "This was much better than having food for breakfast."

She giggled and ran her fingers into his hair. "I would tend to agree." She never wanted the moment to end. But it did when he rolled off her and snuggled into her side.

"Hope, I have a confession to make."

Her heart stopped. Was this where he ended it? "Yes?" How she managed to find her voice was unknown.

"Since the first day I walked into the diner and saw you, I've kinda had a thing for you."

She turned her head so fast to look at him, she was surprised she didn't get whiplash. "What?"

"Yeah. I was attracted to you right away."

Now she was confused. She searched his eyes for any sign of what the hell was going on. Was she now part of his *one-and-done*?

"I never asked you out, well, because we both know my reputation. I figured you were out of reach." He brushed a stray hair from her eyes. "I was also in denial."

She rolled and propped herself up on her elbow. "I'm totally confused as to what you're saying, exactly. Denial of what?"

"That I was attracted to you and not in the same manner I usually am." He scrubbed his hand down his face. "Fuck. I suck at this worse than I figured. I didn't want you to be like the others. I don't want you to be a one time thing."

"I have to confess that I've had this serious crush on you since I saw you." Her cheeks heated. Talk about sounding like a school girl.

His grin widened. "Apparently, I'm a total moron. I missed all the signs."

She sat up. "What makes you think there were any signs?"

"Derrick tried to tell me, so I figure if he noticed then I must have missed it. I also recently discovered that most of the guys noticed it."

Oh, God. She'd been obvious enough that the entire station noticed? Well, she shouldn't have been surprised. After all, Bea had figured it out long before Hope had confessed. "So, what now?"

"How about breakfast now?" He laughed. "I'm starved."

She laughed while he helped her to her feet and handed her a fresh towel. "Lucky for us the casserole reheats well."

"Good. Then maybe we can discuss getting a tree for the holidays. You can help me pick one out?"

"I'd love that."

10

Chance led Hope by the hand across a snowy lot filled with trees.

"What about this one?" she asked.

"Nope. Keep walking." He stopped a moment. "Unless you're tired?"

"I'm fine. I can walk all day." She looked around. "What are you looking for, exactly?"

"These are too small. I have room for a huge tree." He continued toward the back of the lot where not only did the trees get taller, but there were less people. He quickly ducked behind a large Douglas fir and pulled Hope into his arms.

"What are you doing?"

"This." He crushed her to him, their breath steamed the air, and then he kissed her. Explored every inch of her delectable mouth and enjoyed her sweet taste. She responded with a hungry desperation, and her tongue met his, stroke for stroke. Reluctantly, he broke free or he would take her right there in the elements he enjoyed most. But even if not for the prying eyes, Hope wasn't like him. She would freeze.

"I just wanted to kiss you in the great outdoors." Of course, now he had an erection pressing against his jeans. "When I get you back to the house, I plan to make love to you under the tree."

"Is that so?" She raised a brow.

"You object?"

"Not in the least. Can we do it before it's decorated then again after?" She offered a grin that spoke of all the devious things she wanted to do to him.

"I love the way you think. Let's hurry up and pick one."

"Oh, now you're in a hurry?" she laughed.

"Damn straight." He grabbed her hand and practically dragged her past a few more trees until he spotted the perfect one. "This one."

"Are you sure?"

"Yep. Can you hold it while I cut?"

She lifted her chin, a twinkle sparked in her hazel eyes. "I've cut down a tree or two."

"All right then. Let's take this sucker home." He got down on his belly and scooted closer. "Ready?"

"Ready."

He began to saw and, after several minutes, finally broke all the way through the trunk. Hope, like a pro, held the tree upright until the final cut where she let it fall to the ground. Chance jumped to his feet and planted a quick kiss on her lips. She laughed and he undeniably loved the sound of her laughter.

"You really do love the cold."

"And snow. Don't forget the snow. Have you every been dog sledding?"

"No, but it sounds like fun."

"We'll have to go. Cross-country skiing is fun too. Out here in the woods with nature and nothing else. The silence is deafening, if you know what I mean."

She glanced toward the thick tree line. "That sounds like heaven." She looked back at him with longing in her eyes. "I would love nothing more than to share all of that with you."

Chance picked up the trunk of the tree. "Let's head back before you freeze." He was going to have to make sure he took Hope shopping for the proper cold weather gear. No way was his girl freezing on his watch.

My girl.

He was enjoying every second they spent together. The guys at the station were busy ribbing him, but he didn't care. Every time he was with Hope, she brought him calm and his dragon was more settled than the beast had been in its entire life. Chance wasn't stupid and this time he paid attention to the signs. Hope was the one for him. He just had to make sure not to somehow fuck this up. He also had to know she would never fear him, and the thought of her seeing the other side of him scared him senseless. What if she, like Mia, ran from him?

He already knew he would be devastated. He had loved Mia but Hope was different. She had burrowed deep into his soul. Did he love her? Their relationship was so new, and he still kept his emotions guarded. However, he also listened to the beast inside him that screamed Hope was his mate.

"Can I help you drag this beast out of here?"

"Nope. I got this, baby doll."

———

Hope was having so much fun out here in nature with Chance that she half expected it to all end abruptly. She still hardly believed this was all real. That the man she had been wishing would notice her for the past couple years not only finally had, but took her into his home. She still felt guilty, like she was taking advantage and needed to address the issue.

"Chance, there's something I've been meaning to bring up."

"What's that?"

"I really appreciate all that you've done. Opening your home to me and Harley and I'm really grateful. However, I know getting my house fixed is going to take months. I can't impose on you any longer so I've been looking at apartments."

"Are you not happy at my place?"

"Oh my God, very much so. But it's your home and I hate feeling like I'm imposing."

He stopped dragging the tree and stared at her. "It's hard to find an apartment here that allows pets."

She chewed her lip. "I'm finding that out, but I don't know what else to do."

"Well, I was going to bring this up later, but now seems like a better time. Move in with me."

She tilted her head. "I... uh already have, silly man."

He shook his head. "No. I mean you've been staying in the guest room. Move into my room. Stay with me, Hope."

"Oh." She swallowed, her heart pounding so loud she could hardly hear.

"Am I moving too fast?"

Was he? She reminded herself Chance was not David. "No. Not at all. I just wasn't expecting that." She shrugged. "I mean, I know we're having sex, but I would never assume to make that step without you being on board."

"I'm totally on board. I'm on this train for the long haul, Hope." He picked up the tree and started trudging through the snow while she stood there stunned.

Long haul? Did she dare even think what the meaning was behind that? They continued to make their way across the tree lot until they arrived back at the entrance where Chance paid and had the tree wrapped then loaded into his truck. After tying an orange ribbon to the end, he climbed into the cab.

"Want to stop for a bite on the way back?" He started the truck and drove out of the parking lot, turning on the heat as they hit the road.

"Sounds good. We can grab it and head back to your house so we can get the tree inside and into water."

"Hope, my home is yours for as long as you want it to be."

"You are the sweetest man I know."

He glanced at her. "Not all of us are like your ex. Besides"—he waggled his brows—"if you knew what I wanted to do to you right now, you might not think me so sweet."

She laughed. "Perhaps you can show me when we get back. As far as my ex, I dated before him but let's talk about something else." Hope didn't want to live in the past. She was in the now and that included the man next to her who was quickly stealing her heart.

"What would you like to talk about?"

"You." She was about to take a dive off a cliff. "Can I see you shift sometime?"

"Seriously? I guess, but you can't tell anyone as it's forbidden. Unless of course..." he drifted off.

"Unless what? Why is it forbidden?"

"The elders don't want humans to see us shift or know how powerful we really are. They worry it might create chaos so the penalty can be death if we break their laws."

"What?" She shifted in her seat to face him. "That's crazy! Never mind that I even asked. I certainly don't want anything to happen to you." Wow. Talk about some cray cray laws. She didn't even want to try and wrap her head around such insanity.

"We're working to change those laws but things take time. I also don't want to frighten you."

"Frighten me? Why would I be frightened?" Was there something in his past that caused him to believe that?

Chance pulled into the drive-thru of one of the local fast food places. "What do you want?"

"Just a cheeseburger and fries." She was not letting this conversation end. Hope had every intention of picking back up where they left off as soon as they were able.

Chance placed their orders, and a few minutes later, they were back on the road heading to his place.

"Who hurt you?" she asked. No sense in skipping around the issue. Directness was the best way.

"What?"

"You shifted and frightened someone in your past. Who was she?" Her voice remained gentle and she hoped he would share with her.

"Her name was Mia. We were together many years ago. I planned to ask her to marry me"—he sucked in a breath—"so I thought she had better know what I really was. At first, when I told her she thought I was joking. Then when I showed her... The fear in her eyes ripped me in two."

"Oh, Chance. I'm so sorry. That's awful." Her heart broke for him, but a small tinge of jealousy crept in. Chance had wanted to marry Mia?

"That's not even the worst of it. She ran from me and was struck by a car. She took her last breath in my arms."

The pain in his voice brought tears to her eyes. "I-I don't even know what to say. Sorry just doesn't seem like enough. It's obvious you still love her." And that hurt. Would she ever hold the same place in his heart? Suddenly, she realized she was in this deeper than she thought.

"It's been at least fifty years since it happened."

"Is that why you never have a steady relationship?" Her thoughts came back to him asking her to stay with him. What was different about her that he suddenly took the next step?

"Yes."

"And you cannot hold yourself responsible for her death. You didn't send her into oncoming traffic."

They drove the next twenty minutes in silence. When Chance finally pulled into the driveway he unbuckled and reached for her as she opened her door.

"Hope. I thought I still loved Mia, but I lost her so long ago. What I still feel is the guilt of her death."

She took his hand and entwined her fingers in his. "I can't even pretend to understand how you feel, but I'm happy you decided to take a chance on me." She brought his hand to her cheek. "I already know what you are. Have seen the dragon lurking beneath the surface. I've seen fangs suddenly appear then vanish. I'm not afraid of you, Chance O'Connell. I want to get to know every part of you." And that was not a lie.

He pulled her across the seat and into his lap. Kissed her with such desperation and desire he stole her breath. "There's something else you need to know. I've recently discovered that I have a rare gift. I'm what's called a *tamloth* shifter. It means I can not only conjure fire but control every aspect of it."

"That's incredible."

"There's more. That gift didn't show itself until we started seeing each other. You woke something inside me, and the dragon that is my other half wants you, Hope. Wants you forever."

"What are you saying, Chance?" She held her breath.

"That I want you. Every part of me knows that you are the one. I don't want to lose you."

All she could do was blink and wonder if the man in front of her was even real.

Chance got the tree into the house and between him and Hope into the large stand. The thing stood seven feet tall and would be glorious when untied. He wanted to give Hope the perfect Christmas. While she couldn't spend it in her house due to the fire, he would make damn sure she felt at home here.

"Later, I'll get out the decorations and we can light this thing up."

"Sounds like fun. We can drink eggnog with rum while we make a total disaster of this room."

"I like the sound of that. Then I'll get you naked."

"Even better."

"Okay, we should eat our food before it gets too cold." Chance started to head for the kitchen, Hope behind him.

"Chance, we still have unfinished business."

"I know. I threw a curve ball at you. I'm sorry."

"Yes you did, but I'm glad you are honest with me. I like you, a lot."

He took a bite of his sandwich and wrestled with one of the biggest decisions ever. Swallowing, he summoned his courage. "After we eat, I would like to shift for you." He hadn't done so in a while, and he'd been missing his inner beast. The release and freedom he experienced when in his dragon form.

"I can't wait!" She started shoveling her dinner into her mouth, and all he could do was laugh.

"You are unlike any woman I've ever met."

Her smile brightened the entire room. "I'll take that as a compliment." She chewed the last of her burger. "I'm ready when you are."

"All right. I'm going to start you out with a smaller version, one that fits in the house." Chance rose from his seat and Harley lifted his head. Chance noticed the look of concern on Hope's face.

"Don't worry, I won't eat Harley."

She scowled at him. "Not even funny." But the corner of her mouth twitched just a bit.

Chance walked to the middle of the living room while Hope took a seat on the couch. Her gaze focused on him and he pulled in a deep breath. Fear spiked his blood and he knew his hands shook. Hope looked at him.

"Chance, I promise I won't run. I'm not Mia."

He gave a nod and prayed she knew what she was getting into as he called forth the magic that resided deep in his core. Electricity hummed around him as his shift progressed.

Hope leaned forward, excitement in her eyes. "Amazing."

Finally, his transformation was complete.

11

Hope's jaw unhinged as she stared upward. Before her was a creature with sleek black skin that appeared smooth as silk. Green eyes... The same color she often saw in Chance's blue eyes stared back at her. Wings were tucked to the creatures back, obviously too big to spread out. A long tail curled around his body at least three times before coming to rest at his feet. Chance swung his massive head toward the floor and nuzzled Harley who was busy sniffing the dragon's tail.

Chance considered this small? She was dying to see him at full size.

She rose from her seat and with careful steps moved closer. Her hand extended.

"Can I touch you?" Did she really expect him to answer? Yet, in his own way he did by stretching his long neck toward her. She laid her fingers on his snout. The skin so smooth and warm to her touch.

Chance closed his eyes and pushed his long nose into her hand.

"You are the most beautiful creature I've ever seen," she said in a hushed tone. "I simply can't believe you exist. You're truly special."

The air crackled and seconds later, Chance returned to the sexy man she had come to care deeply for. He grinned. "You have no idea how special that was for me. I needed to see that there was no fear in your eyes."

"And, what did you see in my eyes?"

"Wonder, amazement, and maybe a bit of caring."

She stepped into him and threw her arms around him. "There was that and more."

He kissed the top of her head. "I have one more thing to show you."

She stepped back. "What's that?" Would the wonders of this man ever stop?

He took several steps away, gave her a quick glance before he faced the fireplace. Raising his right hand, she witnessed a glow begin to form in the palm of his hand. At first, it started out as a tiny sphere the size of a golf ball, but it quickly transformed to the width of a softball.

"Wow. This must be your new gift." The sphere pulsed with rich colors of red, orange, and yellow. "It doesn't burn you?"

"No. Hold your hand close enough so you can feel its heat."

Hope did as instructed until the warmth from the glowing orb warmed her hand. Chance stared at the ball of fire, and it seemed to pulse even more under his gaze.

"Now touch it."

"Really?" She trusted him and didn't even hesitate. Placed her hand directly over it and experienced a coolness that rivaled the snow outside. "Oh my God! That is simply amazing."

"Now step back." He waited for her to move then launched the ball into the fireplace. A roaring blaze ignited the silent, cold firebox.

Hope only shook her head in disbelief. "Magical."

"I'm still trying to figure all of this out."

She stepped back into him. "I'll help you in any way I can. We'll learn together."

He bent his head and claimed her mouth, and a riptide of desire washed over her. She would never get enough of this man. He was a drug and her addiction. Everything was so perfect. Too perfect and she wondered when it would all end.

———

As Chance plundered Hope's mouth, he was relieved she seemed to accept his other side. The wild, magical side of him including the ability to create fire. He knew this was the first step to claiming his one true mate, but how would Hope accept the thought of becoming his? It wasn't as simple as marrying her. Mating meant her life would change forever. She would gain longevity to her human lifespan, living for as long as he did which could be thousands of years. She would remain young, no longer get sick, and even gain her own special abilities. It was a lot for any female to take in and from the stories he often heard from mated males, it was sometimes difficult to make the transition into the shifter world.

She deepened the kiss, and before he knew it, her fingers wrapped around his growing erection through his jeans.

He moaned. "That's all your fault."

When she looked at him, her hazel eyes burned like molten copper. She slid her hands to the button on his jeans and worked it free. Next came the zipper, and then his jeans and boxers were around his ankles in one motion. Hope dropped to her knees and wrapped her lips around the head of his cock.

He laced his fingers through her thick mane of hair and hissed. "Damn, baby that feels good." She lifted her gaze upward and locked onto his, the tip of his shaft still in her mouth, and he nearly came undone right then and there.

Releasing him, she swirled her tongue just under the rim of his head before leaning back slightly. "I want to give you this. Let me bring you pleasure."

How the hell could he deny her? "If this is what you really want, I'm not one to stop you."

The corner of her mouth quirked. "I didn't think so." Then that wicked mouth slid back over him, her tongue doing things he never thought possible as she nearly swallowed him whole. It was all he could do to hold out. He wanted to make this last for as long as possible. In this moment, both he and his beast were extremely happy.

She moaned around him, the vibration undeniably sexy as hell and the sensation it caused sent a pulse of pleasure through his entire body. His thighs locked tight when she placed her hands on them and began to get down and serious. Working him in into a frenzy that had his balls tightening. Half of his brain wanted to pull her free and bury himself deep inside her. The other...was too far gone to do anything more than tip his head back.

"Baby, I can't hold out any longer." It took every bit of self control not to dig his fingers into her skin as his entire body heated, and he was swept away by his orgasm. Seconds turned into an eternity as his release continued. With a final shudder, he pulled free and lifted Hope to her feet where he claimed her mouth. She smelled of him and tasted the same, and it was all he could do not to claim her. He wondered if this was a battle he would have to fight until she said yes. However, he hadn't really asked her yet, and he had to question what was holding him back. When he looked into her eyes, he never saw fear. Even after all she had been through with her ex, she wasn't afraid of him. Maybe it was time for her to see all of him. The entire full size dragon that he could become. If she didn't run from him then, he would know with certainty she would never fear him. Problem was, he wasn't sure he had the courage to show her what he had shown Mia so many years ago.

"Chance?"

He came back to the task at hand. "You have too many clothes on."

"Perhaps you can fix that?"

The desperation in her voice and the scent of her arousal had him making quick work of her clothing. His female needed him and he would give her anything. Once Hope was naked, he laid her on the floor. The tree towered over them in the corner. Spreading her thighs, he wasted no time in teasing her. Went straight for her honey spot, slipping two fingers inside her, he flicked his tongue across her clit and her hips lifted off the floor.

"So good," she whispered.

It was the encouragement he needed. He worked his fingers

while he licked over her sensitive nub. It only took seconds before she shattered and the taste of her orgasm coated his tongue. His cock was back to full attention and begging to be inside this beautiful woman.

He kissed his way up her body, feeling like the feral male he was. "On your knees, baby."

Her lips parted and then she rolled to her stomach, pushing herself up until her glorious ass faced him. He gripped her hips, rubbed the tip of his shaft along her slickness then entered her in one thrust.

Her head tipped back as she let out a moan. "God, you feel so good. Perfect fit."

Yes, they were. She fit him like a glove and he thrust harder. Faster, until their flesh was pounding together and mewls of pleasure escaped Hope's lips. He reached under her, his fingers tracing a line down her stomach until he reached her sex where he slid a finger over her clit.

"Yes! More of that."

He would deny her nothing and began rubbing the sensitive nub faster until she screamed. Her sex squeezed around him and pulled his own orgasm from his balls. When they finally came back to earth, he leaned over Hope and kissed her shoulder. His fangs ached to sink into her and begin the mating.

Shit, he was so screwed.

———

"Well, how's our fire breathing dragon?" Ash laughed when Chance walked into the station. The shifter was busy helping Halee with gift wrapping. Next week was Christmas, and Halee was trying to get everything ready for the families on the list this year to receive help.

She looked up from her task. "Ha! Now that's funny. How's Hope, by the way?"

"She's fine. I asked her to stop by later with the rest of the donations." He glared at Ash, who was currently wrestling with a role of tape.

"You're a lug. Step away from the tape before you get hurt." Chance shook his head.

"Fucking shit is all stuck to itself," Ash mumbled.

Halee glanced at Ash then rolled her eyes. "For the love of everything holy. Put the tape down and back away. I'm better off doing this by myself."

Ash tossed the sticky mess on the table and walked away. "Fine, I'll go help Reese," he called over his shoulder and then he was gone.

"Poor Reese," Halee laughed.

"Right." Chance picked up the tape dispenser and attempted to rid it of the useless tape. "So, how are the wedding plans coming?"

Halee placed a bow on the package she'd just wrapped. "Good. What's on your mind? It's not like you to ask about wedding planning."

"How did you know Derrick was the one you wanted?"

She set down the package and moved around the table until she stood in front of Chance. "You think Hope is the one?"

He shrugged, not sure how much he wanted to share.

"I just knew. Everything about us felt right, and my dragon was always so settled when we were together. It was a peace I'd never experienced before."

"Yeah. That's kinda what I thought."

"Does she know how you feel?"

"I told her she was the one, but we've not really talked about it."

Halee touched Chance on the arm. "Do you love her?"

"How the hell do I know?" He pushed his fingers through his hair. "Hell, we have only been together for a month."

She sighed. "Perhaps, but you've had a thing for Hope for nearly two years. Denial has been your best friend all this time. All the women are proof of that."

He knew she had a point. "I'm not sure how to ease her into this. I mean, bonding with me will change her life forever."

Halee smiled. "Trust her. Trust yourself." She poked him in the gut. "Most of all, trust this. Our instinct never lies."

"Hey, Chance." Gaelen walked into the room. "Got a minute?"

"Sure." Chance followed the captain down the hall and into his office.

"Close the door so we're not disturbed."

Chance did as asked and worried what was going down that required his captain to have a conversation with him behind closed doors. He couldn't recall anything that might warrant an ass chewing.

"I wanted you to know this since you're involved with Hope Sinclair."

Chance plopped into a chair, his nerves snapping with apprehension. "What's going on?"

"Kadin is talking to the police, and it may be nothing at all. But the night of the fire, a neighbor reported seeing someone enter Hope's house through the patio door."

Chance leaned forward, his composure about to break. "And?"

"And it was right before the fire." Gaelen picked up a stress ball and began to squeeze. "They claim they didn't say anything at first because they assumed it was a boyfriend. However, when questions started getting asked around the neighborhood, they came forward."

Chance's mind was a whirlwind of fury, and it went right to Hope's ex. "You know she has an ex that used to beat on her. Ended up in prison for a stint, but I hear he's been set free." Would the fucker travel this far in search of her?

"Which is why I'm telling you this. You know I shouldn't be, but you need to know that it's starting to look like this fire might have been arson."

Chance's blood ran ice cold.

"Nothing is for sure, and the police are contacting New York to inquire on the whereabouts of this ex." Gaelen squeezed the stress ball so hard it burst, and gel oozed between his fingers. "You know I have no room for any who harm a female, and I can't imagine how you must feel. Just keep your eyes open, but for fuck sake, don't be breaking any laws."

A nod was all Chance could muster, his voice nothing more than a feral growl. He rose from the chair and exited the office, dialing Hope's cell as his boots ate up the floor.

It went to voice mail.

Fuck!

Okay, he needed to pull his shit together. Hope was probably on her way here and in an area of no service. Sometimes it could be spotty up in the forest. He left a message for her to call him as soon as she was able then hung up. There was nothing else for him to do but go to work and wait for her to either call or show up.

12

Hope hummed a Christmas tune as she climbed into her SUV now full of packages. She hadn't been this happy in well... Ever? Chance was a good man and the sex was--knock her socks off--unbelievable. The fact that he was a shifter didn't even factor in for her. He was caring, sensitive and as far as she was concerned, the sexiest man walking. And he belonged to her. She still reeled over the fact he had admitted he wanted her.

Forever.

She wasn't totally sure what it all meant, but hopefully today when she stopped by the station, she could chat with Halee. Hitting the road, she turned up the music and continued down the winding stretch toward town. Thankfully, the pavement was dry today, and no snow in the forecast though the sky was gloomy like it wanted to storm. Hope cranked up the heat to fight the whopping six-degree temperature outside.

As she came to a curve, she tapped the brakes to slow, but the pedal went all the way to the floor. Panic curdled her stomach as she frantically pumped again, trying to gain some pressure. Taking the thirty-mile an hour curve at nearly fifty would be dangerous, and she was picking up speed. With no time to think, she maneuvered into the first curve and was met by a large box truck well over the line. She jerked the steering to avoid hitting the truck and smashed head on into the guardrail. Suddenly, her world spun out of control as the SUV rolled once or twice. The sound of crunching metal echoed in the quiet as pain shattered her body.

I'm going to die.

Her world went black.

The alarm sounded and Chance shoved the entire bag of groceries he was unloading into the fridge. Better everything cold than food spoiling.

Engine 31, Engine 32, Truck 31, Ambulance 32: Accident with injuries, possible roll-over on Miners Drive mile marker thirteen.

When Chance caught the details of the call and the location, his intestines twisted into a knot. It didn't mean Hope was involved. Could be anyone and there wasn't a description of the vehicle. However, Hope would likely be on Miners Drive right about now, and he couldn't stop the dread that spread over him like a dark, suffocating blanket. He geared up, trying hard to remember how to breathe. As he climbed into his spot on engine 31, Reese looked back at him.

"Stop thinking it right now. You have no confirmation it's her."

"Then why do I feel sick inside?"

"Because it's normal," Derrick replied. Chance was glad to have him there.

They rolled out, followed by the rest of the station. Mile marker thirteen was at least ten minutes out and on a winding stretch of road that was frequently used by the logging trucks. It was known for being treacherous, especially in the winter months, but the road had been clear when Chance left for work earlier that morning.

Time was something that slowed to a crawl, and thoughts Chance didn't want to consider punched him in the head. He should never have waited this long to be with Hope. He'd let his own toxic fears rule his life, and now he may have lost out. He closed his eyes and fought to shove everything from his mind. It didn't matter who was in the accident. His job was to serve his community. Save the lives of those he could. Still, he had asked Hope to come to town today. If the call was for her, then it was his fault she was in trouble.

As they approached the scene, local police already had the road blocked and waved them in, pointing to the exact location. The jagged edges of steel, once railing to guard from the fall below, was a clear indicator of what had happened. He was unbuckling before they even came to a complete stop. Everything inside him screamed it was Hope down there.

When he exited the engine, his legs went through the numbing motions of carrying him to the side of the road. While he looked down, his future came to a grinding halt. Shoved against a tree, was a mangled piece of red and silver metal.

He swallowed, forcing everything in his stomach back to where it belonged, turned and ran to the engine. Gaelen shoved out a large hand and stopped him.

"You head down, the crew will grab the gear. I need you to tell us what we've got down there."

"Got it, Captain." Chance didn't hesitate, knowing Gaelen wanted to use Chance's special skill. Every shifter had one and Chance's happened to be the ability to scan a patient. His heightened senses would identify their injuries. Part of him didn't want to know how badly she was hurt. The other half would stop at nothing to find out.

Trudging down the snowy hillside, he couldn't get to her fast enough. Finally, he was able to spot her. Head tipped back and blood trickled from her temple. Chance didn't think his heart could sink any further.

When he reached the beat up SUV, he was assaulted by the stench of coolant and gasoline. A reminder they needed to get her out fast. After a quick assessment, he discovered the roof was only slightly caved in, which was a good sign. However, the front end was pushed so far forward, it was nothing more than a crumpled mess. He approached the driver's door. Glass was busted out of the window and pieces covered Hope. He reached in and laid a gentle hand on her, noting her legs were pinned under the dash.

"Hope, baby I'm here. We're going to get you out."

Her lids opened to narrow slits. "C-chance." Her voice was so low. So broken.

"Shhh. Don't try and speak. I'm going to check your vitals and find out how you're doing. Try not to move." He closed his eyes and focused on the gift of his beast. Heat warmed his fingertips as his senses heightened and gave him the ability to view with the eye no medical professional could. He was able to see Hope's mended breaks and wondered if her ex had given those to her. His anger started to surface and he had to push it away or he'd not be able to function.

He worked from her head, down her chest, through her abdomen and to her legs.

"What did you find?" Halee was beside him and the rest of the crew was there with equipment to open the vehicle.

"Slight concussion. Left ankle is broken and..." he swallowed, the dragon inside him screamed to be set free. Clawed and roared to reach its mate except he and Hope had not mated yet. She couldn't use his strength to heal and he couldn't help her. "Call for an air lift. She has internal bleeding."

"Shit. Okay, I'm on it." Halee's voice faded away.

"Clarke, I want you on a line in case it's needed. Doyle, you and Taylor secure the vehicle so it's stable then get this door off so we can roll that dash," Gaelen ordered.

"I'm going through the back," Chance stated as soon as the men had the vehicle stable. "Hope, I'll be right back." Gaelen handed him a spring-loaded punch, which Chance quickly used to break the back window of the SUV. Brushing away remaining glass, he pushed his way through the opening, into the backseat, and to Hope.

Someone shoved a neck brace at him, which he carefully placed on Hope even though he'd not sensed a neck injury. Next came the blanket, which he began to drape over her. "I'm going to cover you up, baby, including your head, so you don't get hit by any more glass when they remove the windshield." He lowered his face shield.

Somehow, Ash had managed to find room to squeeze between the tree and the passenger door, pushing himself as far into the wreckage as possible, while Evan leaned in through the driver's side.

"Ready," Ash shouted.

Chance turned his head away. "Hope, they're going to break the glass then use a saw to cut it away. It's going to get loud."

Derrick swung his punch, making a hole in the top center, then again in the bottom of the windshield. Flipping the tool, he inserted the saw blade into the opening and began sawing while Evan and Ash made sure the window stayed secure. Derrick made quick work of sawing all the way around until the window was free of its frame, then Evan and Ash each grabbed a side and lifted, walking the windshield out of the way. By the time Evan was back, Ash had procured the hydraulic cutter.

"Hope, you're going to hear some crunching metal, but it will be fine. I'm right here with you." He would give anything right now to trade places with her. Take away her pain, but all he could do was offer reassurance and try not to recall the last time he held onto a woman he loved. A woman who died in his arms.

Hope was not going to die. He wouldn't let her.

Ash started with the passenger side, placed the oversized jaw blade around the top of the A post and twisted the throttle. The blades began to squeeze together, cutting through metal. Once he was done, he moved to the driver side.

Helplessness was a foreign emotion to him. For a moment, he considered saying fuck it and shifting. In his dragon form, he could rip this vehicle open like a tin can. He wasn't afraid of retribution but of Hope seeing his beast so desperate that he would frighten her forever.

Did they even have that much time together? *Stop fucking thinking it!*

Derrick came in with the spreader and began to pry the mangled door from the body of the vehicle. Crunching metal and the hum of the generator became white noise as Chance was forced to watch Derrick continue to manipulate steel. Several minutes passed and the door finally began to give. Ash grabbed the bent frame and yanked, pulling it away while Derrick continued to work the spreader and ply the door. Finally, it broke free. Ash jumped back in with a ram and positioned it between the two posts. Plastic snapped and metal groaned as hydraulics began to roll the dash upward.

"Get some wedges under there," Gaelen shouted.

"Hope, we almost have you. Just a little more."

Derrick shoved wedges to keep everything from dropping back down on Hope, and they finally had enough room to get her out. Halee and Evan rushed in and prepared to pull Hope from the wreck.

"Chance, we're going to pull her out. Do you want to help?" Evan asked.

Chance was thankful for his brothers and their consideration of the relationship that had formed between him and Hope. However, he was also smart enough to realize he needed to keep some distance.

"You guys get her out, I'll take the head on the board though." He watched, his jaw tight while Halee and Evan moved Hope out of the vehicle and onto a board. Once they had her strapped down, they now had to make the climb out. Chance took the head on Hope's right side, while Halee, Evan, and Derrick took up the other three spots then they headed up the hillside. The whir of chopper blades cutting through air assured him that as soon as they reached the road, Hope would be transferred into good hands.

When his boots finally hit pavement, Reese was waiting with the gurney. They loaded Hope onto it and wheeled her down the road where the chopper waited. Before she was loaded inside, he leaned down and placed a gentle kiss on her bruised lips.

"Hang on for me, baby."

Her lids fluttered. "Chance. No brakes," she whispered.

"Save your strength and fight. I'll be back by your side before you know it." He watched as they loaded the one woman who had finally managed to bring balance back to his life into the cargo. The four of them ran back so the chopper could take off, and he nearly ran smack into Kadin.

"You doing okay?"

"Fuck, no, I'm not okay." If she didn't make it, he would never be okay again.

"You're off duty as of this minute. I'll drive you back to the station so you can go to the hospital."

He pulled his helmet off and wiped sweat from his brow. "Thanks, I appreciate that." Chance headed for the truck and climbed in. Kadin climbed into the driver's seat shortly after and they headed down the road.

"How bad is she?"

"It didn't look good." It was all he could get out.

They continued the drive back in deafening silence until Kadin finally spoke. "Look, I'm not sure if this is helpful or not, but if you have had any of her blood. Even a spec. There's a chance you might be able to help her."

Chance swung his head to stare at Kadin. "I've not had her blood."

"Think about it. Not even accidentally? Your fangs have never surfaced when you've been together?"

Despite the pounding in his head, Chance tried to recall any incident. Of course, his fangs had appeared several times and... "Shit! Yes, there was once when we were kissing she ran her tongue over one, but the blood was minimal."

"It might be enough for you to connect to her. I know it's been done in the past, but not to get your hopes up, it's also failed."

Several thoughts ran through his head, but he was keeping them to himself. "She said her brakes didn't work. Make sure that gets checked for me." Something about this whole accident felt off to him.

They pulled into the station, and Chance jumped from the truck, peeling turnout gear off as he went. His mind now reeling with Kadin's words.

13

Chance finally arrived at the hospital after a forty-five minute drive. Hope had been flown to a larger facility where she would get top-notch care. Running across the parking lot, he hurried to the emergency entrance. Inside, he bumped into a nurse.

"Chance. What are you doing here?"

Shit. Jenny had been one of his one-and-done nights last year. Hopefully, she didn't think he was here to see her.

"Hey, Jenny. My girlfriend Hope Sinclair was just flown in."

She blinked, probably in shock at his use of the word "girlfriend."

"Oh. You know the rules. Unless you're on her list of names, I can't tell you anything."

"Fuck, Jenny, of course I know the rules. Considering we only started seeing each other, I'm not on any list."

Her look turned sympathetic. "Does she have family close by?"

He shoved his fingers through his hair. "New York."

She stared at him for several seconds before she started tapping on her tablet. "You should take a visit to the surgical floor. They remodeled the waiting room up there."

He gave a nod. "Thanks. I owe you big time." Walking away, his phone dinged and he dug it out of his pocket as he pushed the button for the elevator.

C hance, I found Hope's phone and it still works. Here is her brother's number. Will be there as soon as I can.

A phone number followed along with the name Eric.

T hanks, Halee. She's in surgery right now I'm guessing. They won't tell me anything.

S o sorry. Hugs, love u.

T hanks. He shoved the phone back in his jacket and stepped into the elevator. It was a quick trip to the second floor where he made his way past the nurse's station, giving a nod as he walked by. No sense in stopping to speak to them, he'd get nowhere anyway.

Shoulders hunched, he walked to the waiting room. At least it was empty because he was in no mood to deal with strangers. He dropped into a chair and helplessness was a foul gritty taste in the back of his throat. He pulled out his phone and proceeded to dial the number Halee had sent him. On the third ring, a male finally answered.

"Hello?"

"Hi, Eric? My name is Chance O'Connell and––"

"What happened to my sister?"

He dropped his head into his hand. "She was in a bad accident. There was internal bleeding, and she's in surgery right now." The words choked him.

"Shit. Okay, I'm going to charter a flight out. Tell me where you are."

Chance gave him the name of the hospital and what city they were in then hung up the phone. It would be at least a three-hour flight before Eric even landed in Minnesota. He leaned back in his chair and closed his eyes, allowing the dragon inside him to stir. His sense of smell heightened until he could break out every tiny molecule. His mate's blood, the coppery scent of her existence caused the dragon to roar in distress. The need to reach her had him breaking out in a sweat as he fought the beast inside him that wanted to be freed.

"Chance? You don't look so good." Bella walked toward him and he was glad for a familiar face. Something to ground him. She took the chair next to him and placed a calming hand on his arm.

"They can't tell me anything. I have no idea if she's going to live."

She gave his arm a squeeze. "You need to have faith. I can't believe she came into your life only to leave you."

"I hope you're right."

"I don't know if I should tell you this right now, but you need to know."

He focused on her brows that were drawn together, and once more his gut knotted into a massive ball. "What?" Jesus, could he take any more?

"I touched Hope's vehicle."

He sucked in a breath. Bella may be all human, but she bore the DNA of her shifter father and with it came a special gift. Isabella Murphy saw the history of any object she touched. Where it had been and who else had come into contact with it.

"What did you see?" His heart rate increased.

"I saw a man tamper with her brakes. I already spoke to the sheriff about it and he's investigating. They have her SUV and are checking it." He knew his body tensed because she squeezed his arm harder and continued, "Before you fly off the handle, you need to hear everything. The sheriff had me go with him to Hope's house, you know just to see if I found anything there."

"And?"

"I know that same man had been there and set the fire. He made it look like Hope left a candle burning."

Chance flew from the chair, ripping free of Bella's grip. His entire body shook with rage. Someone had tried to kill his mate.

Twice.

"Chance, you need to pull your shit together. I can see your dragon lurking below the surface."

"What the fuck do you expect?" The words were no more than a feral growl.

She rose and approached. Did the woman not have a lick of sense?

"I expect you to keep it together, for Hope if nothing else."

He stretched his neck. Rolled his fingers into his palms and pushed back the shift that threatened to take over. "Anything else?"

"No. Other than they are investigating. You have any ideas?"

"Hope had an abusive ex-boyfriend who was just released from prison." He'd stake his life on the fact this guy had come back for revenge. Maybe he'd even seen Hope and Chance together.

"Shit. Do you think it was him?"

"It makes sense. Who else would come after Hope?" He fought his urge to shift and find the son of a bitch that hurt his mate. In order to keep his predator at bay, he paced the floor and watched the clock.

A tall male entered the room, and instantly Chance knew this was Hope's brother. Chance approached. "Eric?

The guy stuck his hand out. "Yeah, you must be Chance."

They shook. "I am. You got here fast."

"Not fast enough. I checked in at the front desk. Hope's out of surgery but not out of the woods. The doctor says next twenty-four hours will be critical, due to the internal bleeding. He thinks he caught everything, now it's up to her to fight."

The man in front of him looked as haggard as Chance felt. "When can we see her?"

"Soon, they said. What the hell happened?" Eric moved to a chair, giving a nod to Bella.

"Oh, this is Bella. She works at the station." When Chance sat back down, he launched into everything he knew, which included Bella and her special gift. Several minutes later, Eric sat with his mouth slightly ajar.

"Wow. I hadn't realized you guys could do such things." He fisted his right hand, working his jaw. It was evident he fought to control smashing his fist into something. "I should have known that fucker would try something, but I thought my sister was safe here." Chance didn't miss the storm that brewed behind the man's eyes because he held the same one. "I failed her."

"Mr. Sinclair?" A nurse stepped into the room.

Everyone jumped from their chairs.

"Can we see her now?"

"Yes. She is in room 203, down the hall. She hasn't come around yet, however."

The three practically ran the woman over to get out of the waiting room and to Hope. When they reached the door, Bella stopped them.

"I think you two should go in. I'll wait out here and give you guys some time."

They nodded and turned to enter the room. Chance's heart couldn't sink any further. Seeing Hope hooked up to machines, bruised and fragile, ripped him in two. As much as he wanted to rush to her side, he allowed Eric to move forward first. Eric took the chair next to the bed, took her hand in his.

"Hey, Sis. I'm here to make sure you get better." He glanced over his shoulder at Chance then back to Hope. "Chance is here too. We're both going to make sure you get out of this bed and back home."

Home. *Shit!* Chance stepped from the room. "Bella, I completely forgot about Harley."

"On it. I'll text the crew. I'm sure someone can pick up the dog."

"Thanks. You're the best." He walked back into the room, knowing he could at least tell Hope her favorite fur ball was being taken care of. When he arrived, Eric rose from the chair and motioned him over.

"You should spend some time with her."

Chance slipped in next to the bed, leaned over, and placed the gentlest of kisses on Hope's forehead. "Baby, I have a confession to make. I can't live without you. I know we've not been together very long, but my heart knows what it wants and that's you. You need to rest and get better so you can come back home to me." Tears, something he hadn't felt since Mia, burned his eyes. "I love you, Hope." There was no denying his feelings anymore and he didn't want to. He had done this to her by asking her to come by the station.

She didn't even stir.

"Harley is fine. One of the guys is going to pick him up."

Still nothing. He'd hoped the mention of her dog might at least bring about a twitch. Part of him wanted to delve deeper and take a look inside and see how she was really doing. The other half was too afraid to find out. All he could do was take her hand in his and realize how small she was. How fragile and so easily lost to him.

"You need to fight, Hope. If you can hear me, squeeze my hand." He waited, prayed, yet his request went unanswered.

———

Hope swore she heard Chance call to her. Maybe even asked her to do something for him, yet he was so far away she couldn't hear what he said. What did he want her to do? Where was she anyway? She tried to remember what she had been doing and suddenly it came back to her in broken pieces. She'd been heading to town and was planning to meet Chance at the station. Something stopped her though.

Pain ripped through her and she seemed to recall falling. Was that right? No. She must be dreaming, because how would she have fallen in her SUV?

Chance was talking to her again, but she couldn't clear the fog in her head. Anger was beginning to take over her emotions because she had no control over her body or mind apparently.

Someone else she didn't recognize started talking to her and suddenly the pain went away and she was floating on a cloud. All the voices became faint as a blanket of warmth spread over her. Light and love loomed in front of her and she reached for it. Wanted to touch it so badly that she called out to it.

"Over here. I'm over here."

The light grew brighter but it didn't hurt her eyes as she thought it should. Instead, it comforted her and she knew it was there to take her someplace else.

"I'm ready to go with you," she whispered. And suddenly the light enveloped her like a warm blanket.

———

I t had only been five hours since Hope was taken to recovery when he received a phone call. The screen said Gaelen Murphy.

"Yeah?"

"I found the fucker and he's bragging about trashing his girl-friend's brakes."

"Where are you?" The dragon was already surfacing as he ran to the elevators and made a hasty exit from the hospital.

"The bastard is right here. Bar several blocks from the hospital."

Not giving two shits, Chance summoned his dragon. The full-fledged, pissed off version that was about to get a taste of human flesh. Thanks to Cearul Murphy, Gaelen's father, Chance had been made aware of an ancient law that stated anyone who attempted to harm a shifter's mate would be tried under shifter law. Did it matter he and Hope were not mated? Not to him or his beast, because he was soon going to rectify that matter.

This fucker was going down.

The shifter high council had already been made aware and laid claim to the human and had made that fact well known among human law enforcement. There was nothing they could do unless they wanted to start a war, and that would be an unwise move on their part.

Chance gave his massive wings a nudge and was airborne, heading for the location his acute senses told him Gaelen was hanging out. After only three minutes on the wing, he was over the top of where he needed to be. Dropping to an alley behind the bar, he shifted back before anyone saw him. No reason to increase his chances of getting caught. That would come later when he introduced David to the several reasons why you didn't ever touch a shifter's mate. He took a second to send a quick message to Bella, telling her where he'd gone.

Striding from his landing spot, he walked in the back door, immediately picking up Gaelen's scent. Ash was with him. He headed for the bar where his two friends sat and took a stool to Gaelen's right. After placing an order for a beer, he looked at his friends.

"Well?"

Gaelen tipped his head. "The guy playing pool and wearing the black T-shirt. He's been mouthing off about his ex-girlfriend and how he tampered with her brakes."

"He's a real piece of fucking work," Ash added.

Chance's gaze shifted to the object of his anger and once the man came into view, his blood boiled. Every scar he had witnessed on Hope physically and internally came back to him. Her words of torment and abuse had his breath coming faster as his heart pounded.

"You know I want to kill him," Chance growled.

"No doubt. So do Gaelen and I, but you know the best you can do is rough him up a bit and scare the piss out of him." Ash chugged the remainder of his beer.

Chance downed his own brew then rose from his stool. "Be prepared to stop me, cuz once I start I won't stop." Then he strode like a thunderstorm across the floor until he was in front of David. The man pinned him with drunken, angry eyes.

"You're in my way."

"Too fucking bad." The two men David had been playing pool with backed up. Apparently, they recognized Chance and were smart enough to not get involved.

"You looking to fight? I have no problem kicking your ass."

Chance ripped the pool cue from David's grip and snapped it like a twig, tossing it to the floor. He grabbed the front of David's tee and in a flash had the man pinned against the closest wall. "Listen up, you worthless piece of fucking shit. I'm not afraid of you, but you are soon going to learn to fear me."

"I'm warning you," David's voice wobbled a bit.

"You're a fucking pussy who only knows how to hurt women. You tried to burn Hope in her home, and when that didn't work, you made sure to tamper with her brakes." He allowed his fangs to descend to full length. "What you didn't count on was me."

"W-what the hell are you?"

"Your worst nightmare." He leaned in until they were nose-to-nose. "I have a fucking beast inside me who promises to kill you should Hope die. My dragon won't care about any laws and sure as hell won't play fair. You. Will. Suffer. I like to play with my food before I devour it."

"You're one of those people." True fear widened David's eyes. Chance let him slide back to his feet before bringing both fists up.

"The only reason I don't kill you now is them." He tipped his head, sensing Gaelen and Ash behind them. "Because I could and your body would never be found. You'd simply disappear. Now, best defend yourself." Chance swung, connecting with David's jaw. The guy's head snapped back, but Chance had tempered his punch so he didn't break the bastard's neck.

David swung, but Chance ducked and landed a punch to David's gut, doubling him over. Before David could recover, Chance swung again, connecting with David's jaw. The crunch of bone under his knuckles gave Chance little satisfaction.

He wanted blood.

Allowing his claws to extend, he grabbed David by the throat again, this time digging into flesh until the man writhed in pain.

"I should fucking kill you, but I know where you will be kept." He allowed a grin to unfurl across his mouth. "I intend to be a frequent visitor, and if you think the shifter authorities will care what I do to you behind those bars..." He laughed. "You can think again."

"I-I swear I didn't mean any harm to Hope. P-please don't hurt me."

Chance's anger was only fueled by David's begging. "Is this what you made her do every time you hit her? Did you make Hope beg?"

"No! I never touched her."

Chance allowed the fire that was now part of him to come forth. His fingers heated and began to sear David's skin. The man's screams had the bar clearing out. "Now, tell me again how you never touched her."

"I'm s-sorry," David sobbed.

"I'm not the one you need to apologize to." Chance was ready to strike again, when he was brought to a screeching halt.

"Chance," Gaelen shouted. "Hospital. Now!"

Chance stumbled backward and Ash moved in to grab David by the collar.

"We'll hold him until a council member gets here."

Chance ran for the back door.

14

C hance walked into Hope's room to the sound of alarms blaring and a flurry of nurses and the doctor.

"What's wrong?" he asked even though he knew Hope was in serious trouble.

"I need you both to leave the room." A nurse pointed her command at Chance and Eric.

"Not a fucking chance in hell," he growled. There was no way he was leaving Hope to whatever fate intended. A hand landed on his shoulder and he tensed. Ready to fight. He'd already left Hope when he should have been here with her. It seemed he continued to let her down.

"Chance, we have to let the doctor take care of her. Her blood pressure is dropping."

Chance whirled to face Eric. "You don't understand, she's my mate. I have to help her. No one else can at this point." He rolled his fingers into his palms and the warm trickle of blood ran between them. He wasn't even sure he could help her, but there was no way he wasn't trying.

The doctor injected something into her IV then looked to Chance. "Are you one of those shifters?"

"Yes." No hesitation, no regrets.

"If you have any connection to Ms. Sinclair, then you should try. I've seen your kind work miracles before and this woman needs one."

He strode to Hope's bedside. "I need this rail out of the way." A nurse rushed forward and lowered the rail, and he slid onto the bed, placed his palms on Hope's abdomen then closed his eyes. He prayed to every ancestor he had that this worked. By all that had been handed down to him there was no connection until a couple mated. Yet, he had to believe Kadin had gained a lot more knowledge over his advanced years.

Chance used his gift to go deep until he saw Hope's beating heart then he followed the flow of blood, the very blood he had a hint of not long ago. Her body was on the verge of shutting down. His fangs lengthened and he bit his wrist and forced a few drops of his blood down her throat and then summoned a partial shift. Wings tore through the fabric of his shirt as they unfurled and spread wide into the room. Gasps came from behind him. A chant spoken in his ancient Celtic tongue fell from his lips as if he had rehearsed it every day of his life.

"Love of my life. Guardian of my soul. I willingly give you everything I am. My heart, my magic, and my very essence." Power flared until it crackled in the room. Heat filled his hands and he worried he might burn her, yet he continued.

"My breath is your breath. With every beat of my heart, yours will follow. My tears..." His power roared into a red-hot flame down his arms until it reached his fingertips. "My tears flow and bring the beginning of life." The mere thought of life without Hope brought forth the single tear that fell and touched her cheek.

Her heartbeat matched his. Each breath they took together, and then the most beautiful thing he had ever seen in his entire life happened. Hope opened her eyes and stared back at him. Flecks of gold and copper fire blazed bright in her hazel eyes.

"Hope." He cupped her face and leaned in to place a soft kiss on her lips. She was alive.

Eric moved in next to them, and even though Chance didn't want to ever let her go again, he moved out of the way.

"Sis. I'm happy to see you. You gave Chance and I a bit of a scare." He looked at Chance. "Thanks. Now I can rest easy that my sister is safe."

Not until they were bonded and Chance was going to make sure that happened.

———

C hance fussed over Hope as if she were unable to care for herself. She sat curled up on the couch, fire crackling in the hearth and Harley on her lap. The lights from the tree glistened like tiny crystals, and she could hardly believe it was Christmas morning.

"I feel fine. Really, you need to stop fussing so much."

He raised a brow. "Most women would like all the fuss."

She grinned. "I love the attention, but I need you to know I feel fine. The doctor cleared me as the most healthy patient he has, all thanks to you." She still couldn't believe that Chance had saved her life. Whatever connection they had before was now even stronger. When had she fallen in love with the wicked grin that curled across his sexy mouth? A mouth that knew every inch of her body intimately. When had she fallen in love with the man himself? Hope thought it might have been the first time he walked through the diner door and sat at her table. It had only quietly grown every time she saw him, until this moment when she thought she might actually burst from the feeling. It was obvious he cared about her. He had saved her life, but she also understood he had a connection to her, which left a burning question that she needed to address. Moving Harley off her lap, she rose and walked to where Chance stood in front of the fire. She wrapped her arms around his neck.

"Thank you for saving me." She still couldn't believe her ex had not only started the fire in her house but tampered with her car. The thought he wanted her dead made her shiver. Chance had reassured her that the shifter council had taken David away and tried him with attempted murder of a dragon's mate. An offense that meant life in prison. A shifter prison.

He pulled her close. "I've waited a long time for you to show up. I wasn't about to let you go."

She studied him, trying to gauge what his response was going to be when she told him how she felt. "So, are we bonded?" She was still unclear what had really happened.

"I only strengthened the bond we already started, but no, we are not bonded as mates."

The explanation disappointed her. She took a slow, deep breath. "Chance, you should probably know that I love you. I think I always have."

He took her mouth in a hard, passionate kiss. His tongue swept across hers and spoke of desperation and desire. He tugged at her shirt until his hands touched her bare skin, and he ended the kiss. "I love you, Hope. The thought of ever losing you makes me crazy." He kissed her again and her body responded, melted into him. Before she could get too comfortable, he took a step back, dropped to one knee and...

"Oh, my God!" Her hands shook as he opened a small black box containing an emerald cut diamond.

"Hope Sinclair, you are my one and only. Since you, there has been no other and never will be. You are my true one-and-done. Will you marry me?"

"Yes. Yes. Yes!"

He slipped the ring on her finger then jumped to his feet, pulling her into his arms. "Merry Christmas, baby. You are the best gift ever."

"Merry Christmas, my very own dragon boy." There was no stopping the smile on her face.

"Boy? Apparently, I am going to have to prove once again I'm no boy."

"I was hoping you'd say that." She leaned in and kissed him, pulling on the button on his jeans.

EPILOGUE

Finding Hope had been the best thing to ever happen to Chance. The second best was when she agreed to become his mate. While Hope didn't want to take away from Derrick and Halee's upcoming wedding, she had agreed to the mating bond right away. They had both decided on a June wedding. He could wait and give her the wedding she deserved. Nothing was too good for his Hope.

"Where are we going?"

"It's a surprise." He'd already dropped Harley off at Bella's so he could get Hope away for the weekend. A light snow fell outside, and the weather was a balmy thirty degrees. He pulled the parka tighter around her before he led her out the back door.

"Your chariot awaits you." He pointed to the four-dog team attached to a sled.

Her eyes widened. "How did you manage this without my knowing?" Hope moved closer, admiring the team of dogs.

"I'm sneaky that way." He held back the fur. "Climb in."

Hope did as he asked, a wide grin on her face. "This is so exciting!"

He threw the fur over her lap then went to the back of the sled.

"Let's go!" And the team moved out, dogs barking with excitement and Hope laughing. The entire scene made his heart swell, and he could hardly wait to get her to their final destination. Chance maneuvered the team through the woods. The quiet of nature surrounded them as the dogs fell into their pace. This was his element, his joy, and he was sharing it with the woman he loved most. Things couldn't get more perfect.

The journey only took thirty minutes but put them several miles into the wilderness where, tucked among towering pines, sat the one room cabin he'd built many years ago. It was his sanctuary.

When he brought the team to a halt, he jumped off the sled and helped Hope to her feet.

"Wow, this looks incredible. Who does it belong to?"

"It's ours. There is no running water but soon you won't care."

She gave him a puzzled look. "Why's that?"

"Because tonight, you become mine forever."

Her mouth dropped open before it turned up into a smile that lit her entire face. "I can't wait."

"Let me show you inside then I'll put the dogs up for the night." He led her to the door then stopped short of the small porch.

"What's wrong?"

"I know this isn't our wedding night, but it's just as important if not more so." He scooped her off her feet and carried her across the porch. Pushing open the door, he took her inside then gently set her on her feet.

"You are such a romantic. I love you." She looked around while he stacked wood in the fire place then used his new found magic to light it.

"Should warm up soon. I'll be right back." He kissed the tip of her nose.

———

The door closed and Hope was left alone in the small cabin. One big room with a fireplace on one end and a king-sized bed on the other. Two chairs sat on either side of the fire and a washbasin was against the other wall. Lanterns adorned the walls and Hope searched for a way to light them. She was quick to locate some matches, which she used to light two of the lanterns. Between them and the fire, a nice, soft glow blanketed the room.

She pulled off her parka, placing it on a hook by the door then kicked off her boots when a wicked idea came to her. Not sure how long it would take Chance to take care of the dogs, she quickly began to undress. The fire had already begun to take the chill from the room but not enough to stop the bumps that prickled her skin. Once completely naked, she crawled between freezing sheets.

"Shit. You better hurry up Chance before I turn into a popsicle." She rubbed her feet on the flannel. Thank God he didn't have satin sheets on the bed.

Several minutes later, the door opened and Chance walked through. When he spotted her clothes on the floor, his gaze went straight for the bed. "You wicked female. You're naked under those covers." He jerked off his coat, not bothering to hang it.

"What was your first clue?"

The man was naked in record time and crawling up the bed toward her like a predator. "I smell your arousal."

"Do you now?"

"I do and I want you. All of you. Will you surrender to me?"

She shivered but this time it wasn't from the cold. It was the from the man who was about to claim her. He had explained the entire process to her, and the thought of his fangs buried in her flesh sent heated desire to her core.

"I surrender." She laid back, allowing the covers to fall below her breasts, her arms over her head. "Make me yours."

————

C hance cupped Hope's breasts then swirled his tongue across a nipple, the sensitive bud hardening under his attention. He wanted to take his time with her, but both he and his dragon were too worked up. The thought of Hope finally becoming his was more than he dare believe. He wouldn't until the bonding was complete. The woman before him was simply amazing. She had absolutely, without a doubt, loved his primary dragon. When he had shifted for her only a few days ago, on a cold, starry night in his back yard, he had been anxious. Hope, however, had not flinched when he summoned the eight-foot black beast whose head was bigger than his pickup. No, she had bravely walked right up to him and kissed him on the snout.

God, he loved this woman.

"I can't take things slow."

"Then don't," she whispered.

He pulled the covers free to reveal her perfectly toned muscles and creamy flesh. Parting her thighs, he slid his fingers through her folds and found her already wet for him. He positioned his cock at her entrance then slid in, careful to allow her time to accept him. But she had other ideas. Gripping his ass, she thrust while pulling him closer until he was planted balls deep.

"We can take things slow later," she whispered in his ear then nipped his lobe.

That was all he needed. Grabbing her wrists, he pinned her arms over her head and began thrusting. He kissed her shoulder, licking the spot where he planned to mark her.

"Do it."

His little mate was an impatient minx, and he wasn't one to disobey her. Summoning his fangs, he struck her in the shoulder. Sinking them deep causing her to cry out in pleasure. The venom he carried pumped into her bloodstream, and the ancient words ran through his head as magic swirled electric in the air. Within minutes, they both cried out their release.

Chance released his bite, careful not to crush her with his weight. "You okay?"

"More than okay. I feel you in here." She tapped her chest. "I don't know how to explain it."

"No need to. I feel it too. We are connected. Our hearts, our breaths, and our souls." He lowered the wall around his emotions. "Do you feel that? How much I love you?"

Tears glistened in her eyes. "I do. I can't believe you are mine."

"Our lives have only begun, baby. We have forever to believe in."

ABOUT THE AUTHOR

Award winning and bestselling author Valerie Twombly grew up watching Dark Shadows over her mother's shoulder, and from there her love of the fanged creatures blossomed. Today, Valerie has decided to take her darker, sensual side and put it to paper. When she is not busy creating a world full of steamy, hot men and strong, seductive women, she juggles her time between a full-time job, hubby and her German shepherd dog, in Northern IL. Valerie is a member of Romance Writers of America and Fantasy, Futuristic and Paranormal Romance Writers.

 Sign up for Valerie's newsletter and be the first to hear about new releases, receive special excerpts and exclusive contests. http://valerietwombly.com/newsletter-sign/

Follow Valerie
www.valerietwombly.com

ALSO BY VALERIE TWOMBLY

Visit ValerieTwombly.Com

An Angel's Torment (Eternally Mated Prequel)

Fall Into Darkness (Eternally Mated #1)

Veiled In Darkness (Eternally Mated #2)

Bound By Darkness (Eternally Mated #3)

Unleash The Darkness (Eternally Mated #4)

Surrender To Darkness (Eternally Mated #5)

Tempted By Darkness (Eternally Mated #6)

Spanish Nights, A Jinn's Seduction

Sultry Nights, A Jinn's Seduction

Taken By Desire (Demonic Desires #1)

Taken By Storm (Demonic Desires #2)

Passion Awakened (Beyond The Mist)

His Burning Desire (Sparks Of Desire)

Rescue Me (Sparks Of Desire)

www.ingramcontent.com/pod-product-compliance
Lightning Source LLC
Chambersburg PA
CBHW030211130726
47898CB00012B/980